101
Witty Stories of
Akbar and Birbal

Wonder House

Wonder House

(An imprint of Prakash Books)

contact@wonderhousebooks.com

ISBN : 978-93-90391-70-7

❋ **This book belongs to** ❋

....

Contents

Akbar Meets Mahesh Das

King Akbar loved going on expeditions to distant places. Once, Akbar and his guards were travelling to Agra, when they lost their way. Hungry and thirsty, they finally reached a junction of three roads. Akbar asked his guards to figure out the correct path, but none of them were able to give him the answer.

Suddenly, they saw a young man coming towards them. Akbar called out to him, and said, "Stop! We are stuck at this junction. Can you tell us which of these roads goes to Agra?"

The man said, "None of these roads go to Agra!"

Akbar got angry and said, "What do you mean? Do you realise that you are talking to the Emperor?" The man smiled and replied, "People go to Agra, sir, not roads. Don't you agree?"

Akbar was impressed with the man's intelligent answer. He smiled and said, "I agree. You are witty and brave. What is your name?"

The young man replied, "Mahesh Das."

Akbar rewarded Mahesh with a bag full of gold coins and said, "Now, tell me, how can I reach Agra?"

Mahesh Das pointed towards the road that would lead to Agra. Before leaving, Akbar gave his ring to Mahesh Das and said, "If you ever come to Agra, come and meet me. Show me the ring, and I will recognise you."

Mahesh Das thanked Akbar for his generosity, and Akbar and his guards left for Agra.

Mahesh Das Gets Employed

Several years had passed since Mahesh Das met Akbar. He lived in a small town. And though famous for his knowledge and wit, Mahesh wasn't wealthy. One day, he remembered Akbar's promise and decided to visit the royal court in search of employment.

But at the gates of the royal court, he was stopped by a guard. Mahesh showed him the precious ring given by Emperor Akbar. Recognising the ring immediately, the greedy guard decided to strike a bargain. He said, "I will let you enter, but on one condition. You must promise me that you will share with me half of the reward that you receive from Jahanpanah."

Mahesh smiled and agreed.He went inside the court, bowed before Akbar, and showed him the ring given to him earlier. The king immediately recognised him and said, "What do you want from me, noble man?"

"Huzoor, I want fifty lashes as a reward," he said.

Everyone in court was stunned on hearing this and assumed that Mahesh Das was a mad man. Akbar asked him the reason for such a strange request. Mahesh said he would reveal it only after receiving the lashes. After Akbar agreed to the unusual request, a soldier thrashed Mahesh Das with a whip.

After the 25th lash, Mahesh Das signalled the soldier to stop and said, "Huzoor, please call the man who guards your palace gate."

Akbar was even more perplexed, but ordered that the guard be summoned inside. As the guard entered, Mahesh Das said, "Jahanpanah, this greedy guard allowed me to enter your court on the condition that I would share half of my reward with him. I wish to fulfil my promise. So, he should receive the remaining 25 lashes."

King Akbar ordered his men to teach the guard a lesson by whipping him 25 times. He then sent the guard to prison for demanding a bribe. He was impressed with Mahesh's wit and decided to make him his chief advisor, and gave him the name Birbal.

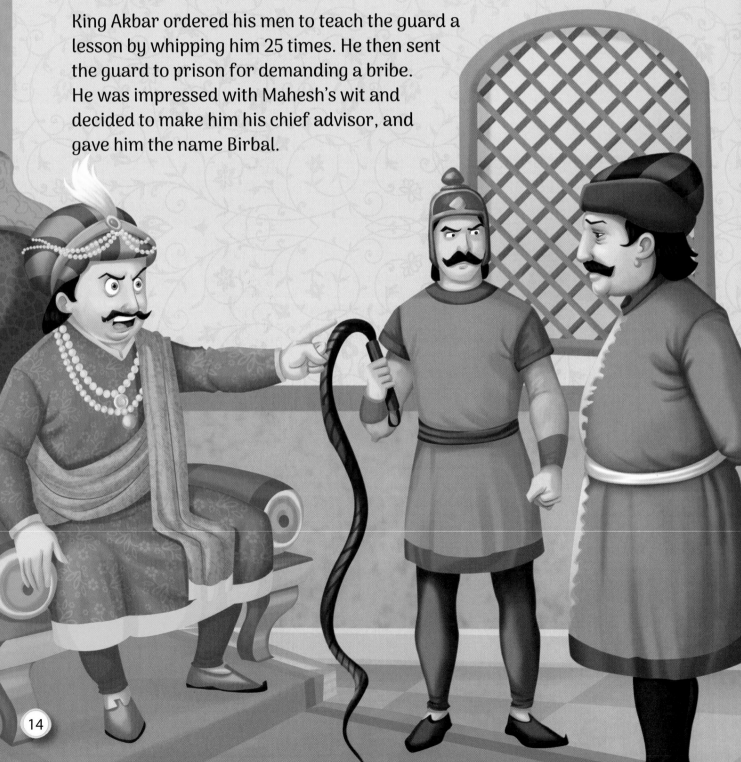

The True King of Persia

When praises of Birbal's wisdom reached far and wide, the Persian king decided to test his wisdom. He invited Birbal to Persia. When Birbal arrived, he was ushered into a large room at the royal palace. Birbal was surprised to see six men, all dressed like kings, assembled there.

One of the ministers smiled and said, "We have heard a lot about your wit. But we have a little test for you, can you identify the real king?"

After observing all six men for a while, Birbal went to one and bowed before him. He truly was the king. The minister asked Birbal how he had managed to recognise the real king.

Birbal politely said, "Only the real king was confident and looked directly into my eyes. The rest were trying to imitate his posture!" This left everyone in awe of Birbal.

The Full Moon and the Quarter Moon

The Persian king invited Birbal to stay with him for a few days. Birbal agreed gladly. A minister approached Birbal and asked, "Oh noble Birbal, how would you compare your Jahanpanah with our Badshah?"

"The Badshah of Persia is like a full moon, while my respected Jahanpanah is like a quarter moon," said Birbal.

The courtiers were happy upon hearing this. The Persian king too was very pleased with the reply, and showered many gifts on Birbal.

The news that Birbal called his Jahanpanah a quarter moon instead of a full moon spread quickly. Emperor Akbar became furious with Birbal as he felt that Birbal had humiliated him in front of another king. When Birbal came back from Persia, Akbar scolded him and said, "How dare you disrespect your king?

You compared me to a quarter moon, but the king of Persia to the full moon! I should punish you for treason!"

Birbal smiled and calmly replied, "Huzoor, please calm down. A quarter moon grows, but a full moon only diminishes gradually. I wanted to tell those people that the glory of your kingdom is increasing every day, while the glory of the Persian kingdom is about to decline. Soon, your fame will overshadow the fame of the king of Persia."

Hearing this, Akbar calmed down and praised Birbal's wits, and welcomed him back to the court.

❋ The Mightiest Sword and the Sturdiest Shield ❋

Once, a merchant who sold spears and shields came to Akbar's court to sell his goods. He showed a shield to Akbar and boasted, "Jahanpanah, this is the sturdiest shield in the world! No weapon can pierce it."

He then showed him a sword and claimed, "This mighty sword can pierce any object." Everyone in the court was impressed. But, Birbal did not like the boastful merchant and said, "I can prove you wrong."

"Impossible!" exclaimed the merchant.

Birbal answered with a smile, "Hold the shield and give me that sword. I will pierce your sturdy shield with your mighty sword. One of your claims has to be wrong!"

Akbar appreciated Birbal's quick wit and dismissed the merchant from the court.

The Cost of Justice

 King Akbar liked to test Birbal with questions and riddles. One day, he asked Birbal, "If given a choice between a gold coin and justice, what would you choose?"

"Undoubtedly, the gold coin," said Birbal with a smile.

Everyone in the court, including Akbar, was surprised. A few courtiers who were jealous of Birbal complained that Birbal had become greedy. The king was disappointed with Birbal's choice. He asked, "Why wouldn't you choose justice, Birbal?"

Birbal said, "Huzoor, justice is already available to everyone in your kingdom. That's why I would choose a gold coin."

The courtiers applauded Birbal's witty answer. Akbar too was pleased with his answer and rewarded him with several gold coins.

A Little Less and a Little More

Once, Birbal's ten-year-old daughter accompanied him to the royal court. King Akbar was pleased to meet the sweet little girl. He treated her affectionately and gave her many sweets. Akbar asked her, "My dear little girl, do you know Persian?"

"A little less and a little more," she replied. After hearing the answer, Akbar was confused and turned to Birbal for further clarification.

Birbal said, "Huzoor, my daughter meant that she knows Persian lesser than those who are fluent in Persian, but more than those who don't know it at all."

Hearing this, Akbar laughed loudly and said, "Birbal, your daughter has certainly inherited your wit."

Birbal was proud of his daughter and thanked King Akbar for his generous praise.

The Perfect Portrait

Harinath was a gifted painter who lived in Akbar's kingdom. One day, a rich merchant approached him to get a portrait made. Hoping to make a good fortune, Harinath happily went to the merchant's house. He stayed there for several days to paint the perfect portrait. Finally, Harinath finished the portrait and showed it to the merchant.

The merchant thought, "This painting is indeed beautiful, but if I appreciate it, I will have to pay Harinath. Rather, I should criticise it and get it for free."

The miserly merchant started pointing out flaws in the painting. Harinath painted another one, but the merchant was still not satisfied. Harinath realised that the miserly merchant won't pay him, so he approached Birbal for help, who agreed to help him.

Birbal summoned the merchant and asked him the reason for not paying. The merchant replied, "I want a portrait that looks exactly like me, but Harinath is unable to paint it."

Birbal asked Harinath to paint one last portrait. He asked the merchant to come back the next day and pay Harinath if he liked the portrait. Both of them agreed and left.

The next day, the merchant reached Birbal's house. He saw that the painting was covered with a cloth. The merchant removed the cloth but was surprised to see his reflection in a mirror. The merchant was angry. Birbal said, "Don't you think it looks exactly like you?"

The merchant realised that he had met his match. He apologised to Birbal and paid Harinath a handsome sum for the portraits.

The Noble Beggar

King Akbar once asked Birbal, "Oh my wittiest courtier, is it possible to be the noblest and the lowest at the same time?"

"Yes, Huzoor," asserted Birbal.

Akbar asked him to bring to his court such a person who is both noble and belongs to the lowest strata of society. Birbal nodded and left the court. Within a couple of minutes, he returned with a frail-looking beggar and said, "Jahanpanah, this man belongs to the lowest strata among all your subjects in the entire kingdom."

Akbar asked, "Okay, but how is he noble?"

Birbal replied, "He has got an audience in the royal court of the greatest Mughal ruler, King Akbar. This makes him the noblest."

Once again, King Akbar praised Birbal and gave several gifts to the beggar.

The Limping Horse

Once upon a time, a prized horse started limping in King Akbar's kingdom. Initially, everyone thought it could be a minor injury or a fracture. Numerous vets were called for its treatment, but no one was able to diagnose the ailment.

Finally, the stable owner approached Birbal and asked for his help. Birbal went to the stable and inspected the horse. He then asked the stable owner, "Does the trainer of this horse limp?"

The owner nodded and replied, "The trainer of this horse met with an accident and now walks with a limp. But how did you know that?"

Birbal clarified, "Your horse is only imitating its trainer. We often imitate those we admire."

The stable owner thanked Birbal and ordered that the trainer be changed. Once the trainer was replaced, the horse stopped limping.

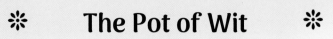

The Pot of Wit

Once, after a disagreement, King Akbar became furious with Birbal and asked him to leave the court. Birbal obeyed and went to a village far away. There, he began working as a farmer, without revealing his true identity.

Akbar began regretting his actions within a few days. So, he devised a plan to find Birbal. He immediately sent an order to every village, asking the villagers to fill a pot with wit and send it to court. If they can't fill the pot with wit, they must fill it with jewels.

When Birbal heard the announcement, he assured the villagers, "I will fill the pot with wit in a month."

He took a pot in his arms, and headed to a watermelon farm. There, he chose a small watermelon and placed it inside the pot, without cutting it from the vine. He nurtured the plant carefully.

Soon, the watermelon grew in size and it became impossible to remove it from the pot without damaging either. Birbal finally cut the vine when the watermelon fit the pot entirely. He then sent the pot to the king's court with a message saying, "Your Majesty, please remove the wit from the pot without cutting it or breaking the pot."

Akbar instantly knew that only Birbal could reply in such a witty manner. He personally visited the village from which the message came, and brought Birbal back to the court.

The Disputed Well

Iqbal was a shrewd farmer living in Akbar's kingdom. He owned a garden which had a well in the corner. His neighbour was also a farmer, who wanted to purchase the well to irrigate his fields. Iqbal sold the well to his neighbour for a handsome sum. The next day, the neighbour was surprised to see Iqbal drawing water from the well.

The neighbour shouted, "I own that well now! Why are you drawing water from my well without my permission?"

However Iqbal did not pay any attention to his neighbour and kept drawing water from the well. This led to an argument between the two, and they reached King Akbar's court to settle their dispute.

Akbar asked Birbal to resolve the dispute.

Birbal enquired of Iqbal, "You have sold the well to this farmer. Why do you still draw water from it?"

Iqbal cunningly answered, "I sold the well to the farmer, not the water. I can still use the water!"

Birbal said, "So, you claim that the water in the well is yours? But how can you keep it in another farmer's well without paying rent? You must pay rent to your neighbour!"

Stunned, Iqbal couldn't argue further. Scared of punishment, he begged Akbar and Birbal for forgiveness and promised not to use water from the well again. The neighbour thanked Birbal and left.

✻ Birbal's Khichdi ✻

Once, King Akbar and Birbal were walking beside a lake when Akbar said, "I wonder if a person will agree to stand in the lake for an entire night, in this freezing winter, if I offer him a handsome reward."

Birbal replied, "Yes, Your Majesty. If a person is desperate for money, he will agree to do this task."

The king ordered him to prove his statement. The next day, Birbal came to the court with a poor priest. He claimed, "Your Majesty, this priest is very poor and will stand in the lake the whole night."

Akbar promised to give the priest a hundred gold coins if he successfully completed the task. The poor priest was happy and agreed instantly.

The priest stood shivering in the cold lake all night long. The next morning, he returned to the court to receive his reward. Akbar said to the priest, "How did you manage to stand in the freezing water all night?"

The innocent priest replied, "Jahanpanah, I saw a faint glowing light coming from your palace. It gave me the strength to stand in the cold water."

Akbar shouted, "Is that so? Well, then you do not deserve the reward! You cheated. The light from the palace gave you warmth."

The poor priest went back empty-handed. Birbal tried to convince the king to change his decision, but failed. The next day, Akbar wanted to go hunting, but Birbal wasn't present in the court. He sent soldiers to Birbal's house to summon him to the court.

Birbal said to the soldiers, "Tell Jahanpanah that I will return to court once I finish cooking my khichdi."

The soldiers conveyed the message to Akbar. He was intrigued and went to Birbal's house himself. He saw that Birbal had lit a fire but the utensil was hanging very far away from it.

Akbar became furious and said, "You will never be able to cook khichdi this way, Birbal! The utensil is too far from the fire."

Birbal replied calmly, "Huzoor, if the priest can receive warmth from a light that was placed so far away from him, then I am sure that I will be able to cook my khichdi, which is relatively near to the fire."

Akbar then realised his mistake. He called the poor priest the next day and rewarded him with two hundred gold coins.

The Loyal Gardener

Once, Akbar was taking a stroll in his garden, when he suddenly stumbled upon a rock and fell. Akbar was angry and ordered the execution of the gardener, as he felt that his fall was the gardener's fault. The gardener went to Birbal for help. Birbal whispered a plan in his ears.

The next day, the gardener was asked his last wish before his execution. He said, "Please take me to King Akbar!"

After reaching the court, the gardener spat on Akbar's feet. Everyone at the court was outraged, but Birbal rushed to the gardener's rescue and said, "Your Majesty, this is the most loyal gardener in your kingdom. He spat on your feet to make people think that you killed a poor gardener for a valid reason."

Akbar understood Birbal's point and pardoned the innocent gardener. The gardener profusely thanked Birbal for saving his life.

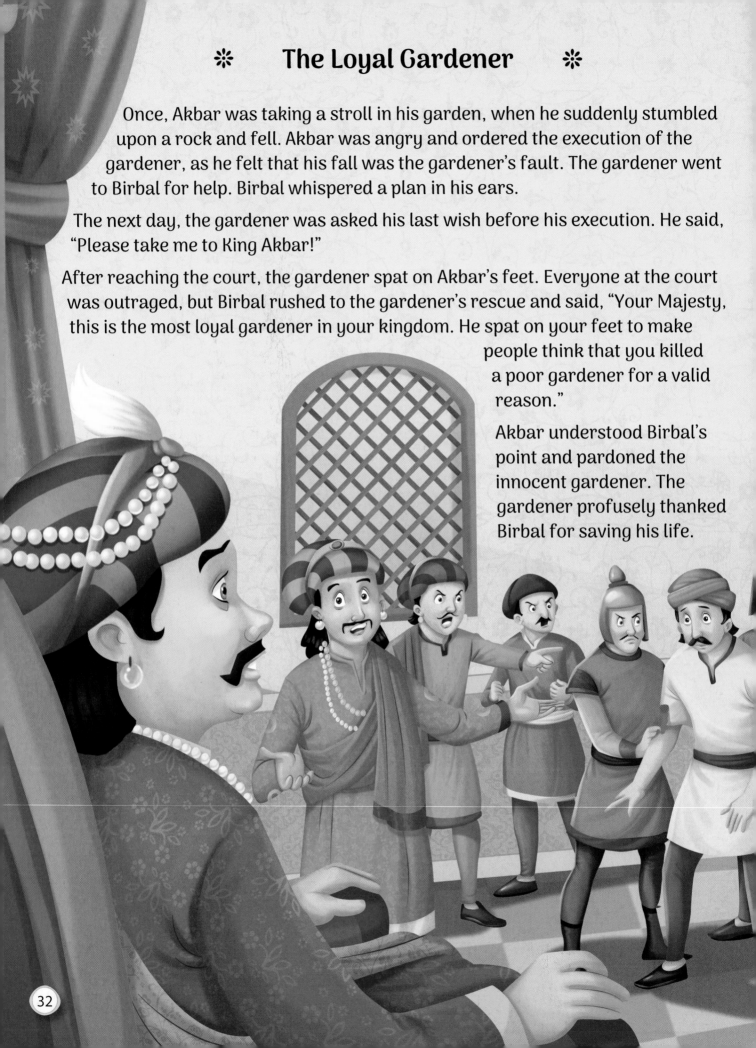

❋ Birbal the Servant ❋

One day, Akbar and Birbal were riding through the kingdom when they passed by a brinjal patch. "Brinjals are ugly looking vegetables. I don't like them at all!" exclaimed the king.

"I agree, Your Majesty. Brinjals don't even taste good," replied Birbal.

A few weeks later, when Akbar and Birbal were having lunch, the chef brought a plate of brinjals. The king was delighted to eat the dish and said, "Oh, what a delicacy! Brinjals taste so good! What do you say, Birbal?"

"Yes, Your Majesty! They taste amazing," replied Birbal.

On hearing this, Akbar asked him, "But the other day, you said that you don't like the taste of brinjal. Why did you change your opinion?"

Birbal smiled and answered, "Your Majesty, I am your servant, and owe no loyalty to brinjals!"

Akbar laughed at Birbal's humorous reply.

The King's Whiskers

One fine morning, King Akbar was sitting in his royal throne when a question struck his mind. He asked his courtiers, "Tell me, courtiers, what punishment should I give to a person who pulls my moustache?"

A minister replied, "Your Majesty, that person should be beheaded!"

Other courtiers too suggested many cruel punishments for the person who dared insult their king. Later, when Akbar met Birbal, he asked, "Birbal, what do you think?"

Birbal thought for a while, and then said, "Your Majesty, that person should be rewarded with sweets!"

"What? Why?" asked Akbar.

Birbal politely answered, "Jahanpanah, the only person who can dare to pull your whiskers is your grandson!"

Thinking about his naughty grandson, Akbar loudly laughed at Birbal's answer and awarded him several gold coins.

❋ The Fake Mother ❋

One day, two women came to King Akbar's court with a baby. The first woman said, "Jahanpanah, I have come to your court for justice. This woman is trying to steal my child."

The second woman said, "No, Your Majesty. This child is mine. I am his mother!"

Akbar asked Birbal to resolve this dispute. Birbal addressed the women saying, "To end this fight, we should split the child into two, so that each of you can keep one part of him."

Suddenly, the second woman shouted, "No, please don't split the child into two. This woman can keep the child!"

Birbal smiled and announced, "The child belongs to the second woman! Only a mother can make such a great sacrifice to protect her child."

The first woman was sent to prison and the baby was handed to the real mother. All the courtiers praised Birbal's wit.

The Crows in the Kingdom

Emperor Akbar loved strolling in the royal gardens. One day, he was taking a walk in the garden with Birbal and a scholar from another kingdom. It was a beautiful morning, and many birds were chirping around them.

Jealous of Birbal's fame, the intelligent scholar decided to belittle Akbar's favourite courtier. He asked Akbar, "Your Majesty, can you tell me how many crows there are in your kingdom?"

Akbar was surprised to hear this question. He turned to Birbal and ordered him to answer the man's question. Birbal thought for a moment and said, "I will need a day to count the birds and will give you the exact answer tomorrow."
Birbal bid them farewell and left the garden.

The next day, Birbal went to the court and announced, "Your Majesty, there are 95,463 crows in your kingdom."

Akbar was amazed to hear such a precise answer. The scholar was still not convinced. He asked Birbal, "Okay! But what if there are more crows?"

Birbal didn't hesitate for even a moment. He said, "If there are more crows in the kingdom, it means that some crows from the neighbouring kingdoms have come to visit their relatives."

The scholar retorted, "And what if there are fewer crows?"

Birbal smiled and answered, "Then, some of the crows from our kingdom must be visiting their relatives!"

On hearing Birbal's retort, Akbar started laughing loudly and praised Birbal for his quick wit, while the scholar was left tongue-tied.

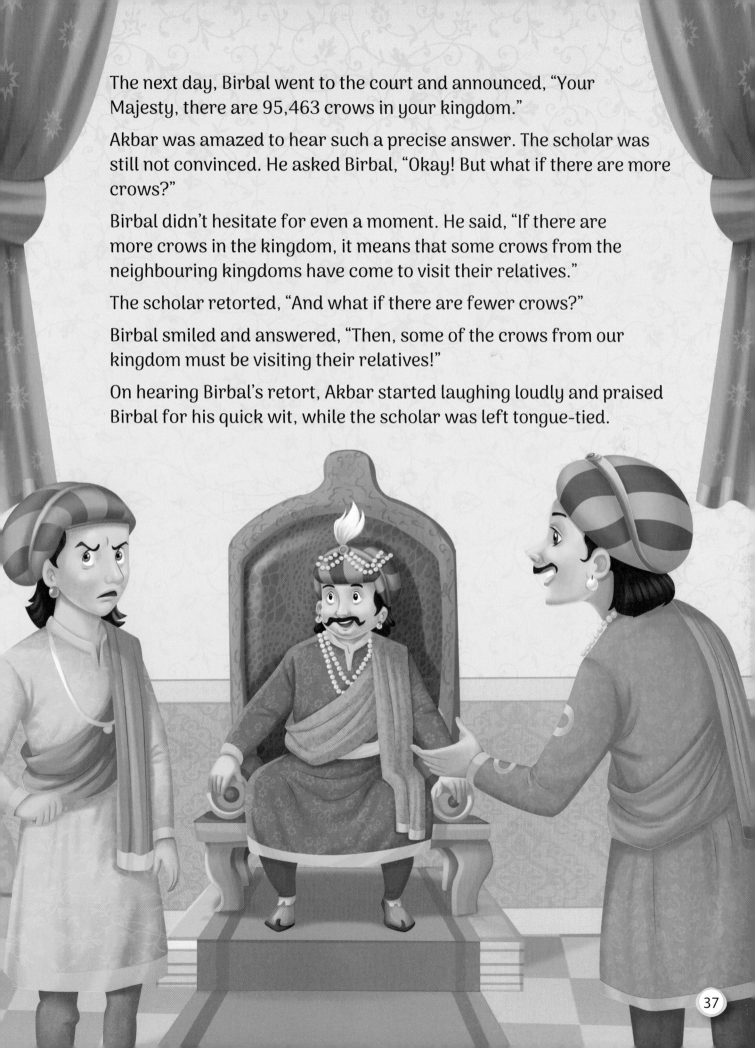

The Magical Stick

Once, a local merchant approached Birbal for his advice. He anxiously said, "Sir, help me. Someone steals money from my home on a daily basis."

Birbal went to the merchant's house, called all the servants, gave them a wooden stick each, and said, "These are magical sticks. The stick will grow by two inches during the night if you have stolen money from your master."

The next day, Birbal inspected every stick and pointed out the thief immediately. The astonished merchant asked Birbal how he caught the thief. Birbal replied, "These were ordinary wooden sticks. But this man cut his stick short by two inches, fearing that it will grow two inches in the night."

The merchant fired the thief and thanked Birbal.

A Tale of Tongues

Once, a priest visited Emperor Akbar's court and said, "Your Majesty, can any of your courtiers guess my mother tongue? If they fail to guess correctly by tomorrow, I will assume that I am superior to them all!"

The courtiers conversed with the scholar in various languages. He spoke all of them fluently, and they could not guess his mother tongue. Birbal was then asked to guess the answer. So, he went to the priest's house at night, dressed like a ghost. The priest woke up with a start and screamed, "Jai Jagannath!"

Birbal took off his costume and said, "You are from Odisha! A man always speaks his mother tongue when in distress!"

The priest accepted his defeat and congratulated Birbal for his wit. The next day, Akbar rewarded Birbal for creating a good impression of the kingdom in front of the scholar.

❋ Birbal Goes To Heaven ❋

Several of Akbar's courtiers were jealous of witty Birbal's popularity. One day, they hatched an evil plan to get rid of him permanently. They bribed the royal barber with a huge sum to execute their plan.

The next day, while shaving Akbar's beard, the barber said, "Jahanpanah, I saw your ancestors in my dream, they were all really sad. Why don't you send someone to heaven to enquire about their well-being?" Akbar was worried to hear that his ancestors were sad and replied, "How can anyone go to heaven and come back alive?"

The barber said, "I know a magician who can send people to heaven without killing them. If the person is smart, he will find a way to come back."

Akbar was excited and wanted to meet the magician. The barber brought the magician to the king's chambers. The magician reassured Akbar that he would use his magic to send one person to heaven alive. He asked the king to choose the wisest man for the job.

Akbar was elated. The next day, he summoned Birbal to the royal court and said, "Birbal, are you willing to do anything for your king?"

Birbal replied, "Yes, Jahanpanah! I'm ready to do anything for you."

Akbar was relieved and said, "Excellent! I want you to go to heaven and enquire about the well-being of my ancestors."

Birbal was taken aback by this strange request but he decided to remain calm and composed.

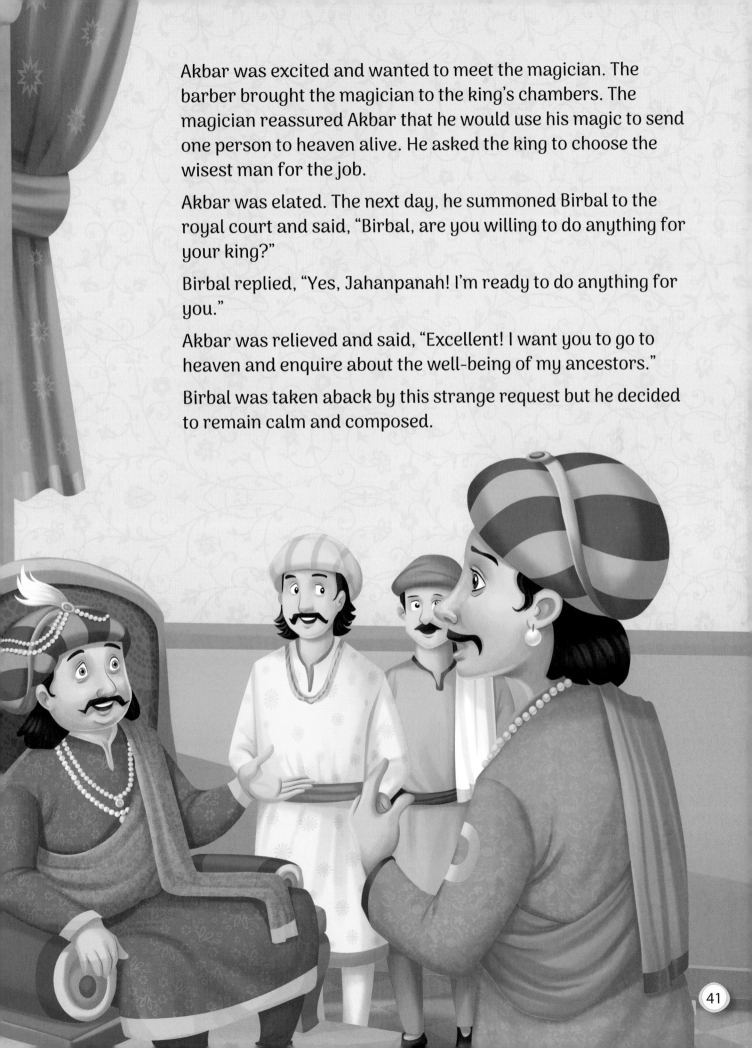

Akbar told Birbal about his conversation with the barber and the magician. Birbal looked around and saw happy faces. He realised that several courtiers had conspired with the barber to get him killed. He then calmly replied, "Huzoor, it will be an honour. But I have two conditions. I need a lot of money to prepare for the travel. Secondly, I want the ceremony to take place near my house, exactly after one month."

Akbar agreed instantly. He sent a huge sum of money to Birbal's house and gave him one month as a leave of absence to prepare for the journey. On the appointed day, Akbar, accompanied by the magician and the barber, reached Birbal's house. The stage was set, and Birbal jumped into a pyre as the magician chanted hymns. Huge flames and smoke filled the surroundings.

Birbal Returns from Heaven

The cunning courtiers were happy to see their evil plan work flawlessly. They thought that they had finally succeeded in defeating Birbal and killing him. However, Birbal had planned his escape. He had utilised the money sent by Akbar to build a secret tunnel from the ritual site to his home. Using smoke as a cover, Birbal entered the tunnel and reached his home safely. Though his clothes were torn and burnt, his face had a cunning smile on it. Birbal stayed hidden inside his house for a month and did not shave his beard.

Days passed, and Akbar started getting restless waiting for Birbal. Meanwhile, the courtiers secretly celebrated Birbal's demise. After a month, Birbal went to the royal court. Akbar was extremely happy to see him, while the courtiers couldn't believe their eyes.

Akbar eagerly asked Birbal, "Did you meet my father? How is my grandfather?"

Birbal smiled and said, "Jahanpanah, your ancestors are doing well in heaven, but they lack a barber. Look at my beard. Your ancestors also have long beards. They have asked me to request you to send a barber for them."

The king immediately summoned the royal barber to court and told him about Birbal's experience. He ordered the barber to go to heaven. The barber got scared. Falling to his knees, he revealed the evil plan to kill Birbal and named the other co-conspirators. He begged for forgiveness, but Akbar sent all of them to prison and rewarded Birbal for his bravery and wit.

The Most Beautiful Child

Akbar and Birbal were travelling through their kingdom one day, when they noticed a woman calling her son the most beautiful child in the world. King Akbar asked Birbal, "Why is this woman calling her son the most beautiful child? He looks normal to me."

Birbal replied, "Your Majesty, to a parent, his or her child is indeed the most beautiful!" Akbar was not convinced. So, the next day, Birbal asked one of the courtiers to find the most beautiful child and bring him or her to court.

The courtier returned with his own son. Akbar asked him why he had brought his own son. He meekly replied, "Your Majesty, I asked my wife to help me find the most beautiful child in the kingdom. She said that it was our son, I too agreed. So, I brought him here."

Akbar realised his folly and gave the child lots of sweets.

Greater Than God

Once, a merchant came to Akbar's court. As he entered, he started singing Akbar's praises. Since he wanted to sell his goods to the royal court, he flattered Akbar and said, "Jahanpanah, you are greater than God."

Akbar knew that the merchant was trying to flatter him, but he wanted to test Birbal. So, he turned to Birbal and asked, "What do you think, Birbal?"

Birbal smiled and said, "Yes, huzoor, this is the truth."

Akbar was astonished and asked for an explanation.

Birbal added, "Jahanpanah, you can do one thing that God cannot. You can expel anyone from your kingdom. But God cannot expel anyone because the whole universe is His kingdom."

Akbar and his courtiers applauded Birbal's answer, with which he had managed to flatter Akbar and not offend God, at the same time.

Counting Stars

One day, a minister complained to Akbar saying, "You praise Birbal all the time. But I will accept Birbal's superior wit only if he can answer my question."

Akbar gave him permission to do so. The minister asked Birbal, "Can you tell me the exact number of stars shining in the sky?"

Birbal promised to tell him the answer the next day, as he wanted to count the stars during the night.

The next morning, Birbal brought a sheep with him to the court. He said to the minister, "The number of stars in the sky is equal to the number of hair on this sheep. You can count them if you want to verify my answer."

Knowing that there was no way to prove Birbal wrong, the minister accepted his defeat. Akbar was impressed with Birbal's wit and rewarded him with a bag of gold coins.

A Marriage of Seas and Rivers

King Akbar once ordered Birbal to leave the court because he was angry with him. Birbal left the court quietly. But soon, the king started missing Birbal's advice. He asked his courtiers to find Birbal, but no one could find him. Finally, Akbar decided to issue a challenge that only Birbal could win. He sent a message to all the kings of the neighbouring kingdoms saying, "Emperor Akbar is looking for the perfect match for his sea. Send your rivers to him."

He soon received a reply from a neighbouring kingdom, saying, "We're ready to send our rivers, but ask your sea to receive our rivers midway."

King Akbar understood that only Birbal could come up with such a witty reply. He went to the neighbouring kingdom, and upon finding Birbal there, he asked him to re-join the court. Birbal agreed and came back with Akbar.

Emperor Akbar's Ring

One day, Akbar lost a precious ring. When Birbal came to court, Akbar said to him, "I lost the precious ring that my father had given me. Can you help me find it?"

Birbal knew that someone in the royal court must have found the ring and did not report it to the king. He replied, "Jahanapanah, I can find the ring immediately. The thief is present in this court and has a twig in his beard."

On hearing this, a courtier got startled and began cleaning his beard. Seeing the action, Birbal pointed towards him and said, "Guards, search this man. He must have Jahanpanah's ring."

The soldiers frisked the courtier and found the ring. Curious, Akbar asked Birbal how he knew about the twig. Birbal laughed and explained, "Your Majesty, there was no twig. I tricked the guilty thief into revealing himself by making him look for this imaginary twig." Thoroughly impressed, Akbar rewarded Birbal and dismissed the greedy courtier from his court.

To Count or not to Count

One day, Akbar was having lunch at Birbal's home. After having their meal, King Akbar asked Birbal, "Can you tell me how many bangles there are on your wife's wrist?"

Birbal shrugged and said, "I have no idea."

Akbar teased Birbal, "I'm surprised! You see her hand every day, yet you failed to notice the number of bangles she wears." Birbal simply smiled in response.

Akbar and Birbal went back to the palace. After descending some stairs there, Birbal asked Akbar, "Huzoor, you climb this staircase every day. Can you tell me how many steps there are in it?"

King Akbar did not have an answer. He replied, "I get your point, Birbal. We should always focus on the important aspects of life."

❋ Fear or Respect? ❋

Akbar and Birbal were taking a stroll, when Akbar said, "Birbal, my courtiers are obedient to me. They love and respect me. This makes me proud."

On hearing this, Birbal smiled and added, "Yes, Jahanpanah, they love and respect you, but they also fear you." The king was not pleased to hear this, and he asked Birbal to prove his statement.

Birbal then made an announcement in the court, saying that King Akbar is going for a hunt and has ordered his officials to bring some milk and pour it into a step-well in the courtyard before dawn. The next day, when Akbar went to the courtyard, he was surprised to see that the well was, in fact, filled with water, and there was not a single drop of milk in it.

Birbal explained to Akbar, "Look Jahanpanah, everyone thought that they could get away by pouring water in the well. They were counting on others to pour milk in the well. They believed that they would never be caught."

Birbal then made another announcement saying that Akbar had asked his officials to again pour milk in the step-well in the courtyard, and this time, he would personally check after returning from his hunt.

That evening, when Akbar returned from hunting, he saw the well overflowing with milk. Birbal said, "Huzoor, all courtiers poured milk in the well since you announced that you would check the well yourself. See? It is evident that they fear you."

Akbar agreed with Birbal and said, "Fear is also important for upholding law and order, else people won't hesitate to break the law."

The Marriage Procession

Many courtiers in Akbar's court envied Birbal. One day, Akbar, Birbal and other ministers were standing on the palace's rooftop. One of the ministers complained to Akbar, "Jahanpanah, you give more importance to Birbal's suggestions, while you ignore your other ministers and their advice."

Akbar was worried to hear that his ministers thought he was partial towards Birbal. He decided to prove to the courtiers why he valued Birbal's decisions and advice so much.

Suddenly, he saw a marriage procession passing below. He instructed a minister, "Go and check whose marriage procession is passing through the city gate."

The minister came back after speaking to the groom and proudly stood in a corner.

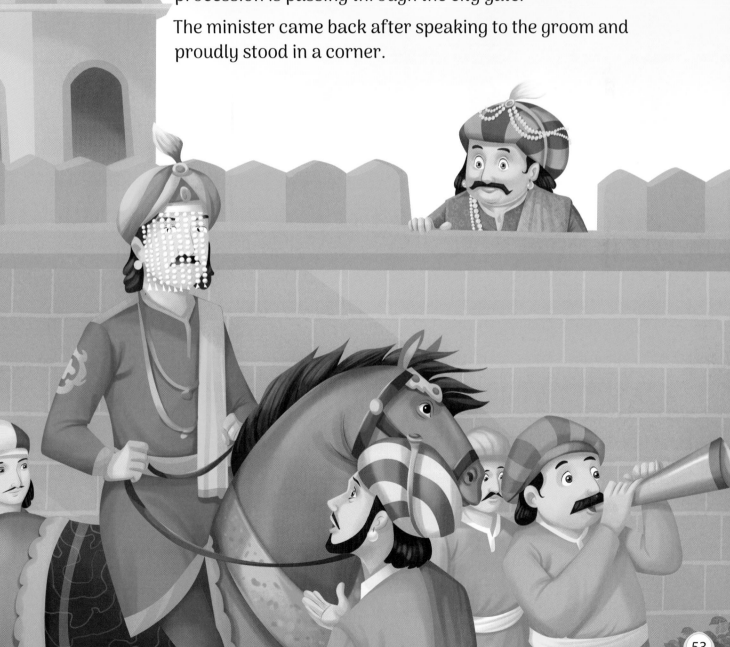

Akbar then ordered Birbal to make the same enquiry. Birbal made his enquiries and returned quickly. Akbar then looked at the minister and asked, "Tell me, where is the couple going?"

The minister was surprised. He protested meekly, "Huzoor, you just asked me to find out whose marriage it was! How can I know where they're headed?"

Akbar then asked Birbal the same question. Birbal confidently replied, "Jahanapanah, they are going to Allahabad."

Akbar turned to the minister and explained, "Do you now understand why I value Birbal and trust his advice? He does not simply complete a task but uses his intelligence to understand all aspects of the task. He anticipates problems and is always ready with solutions."

The minister finally understood Birbal's importance and apologised for his behaviour.

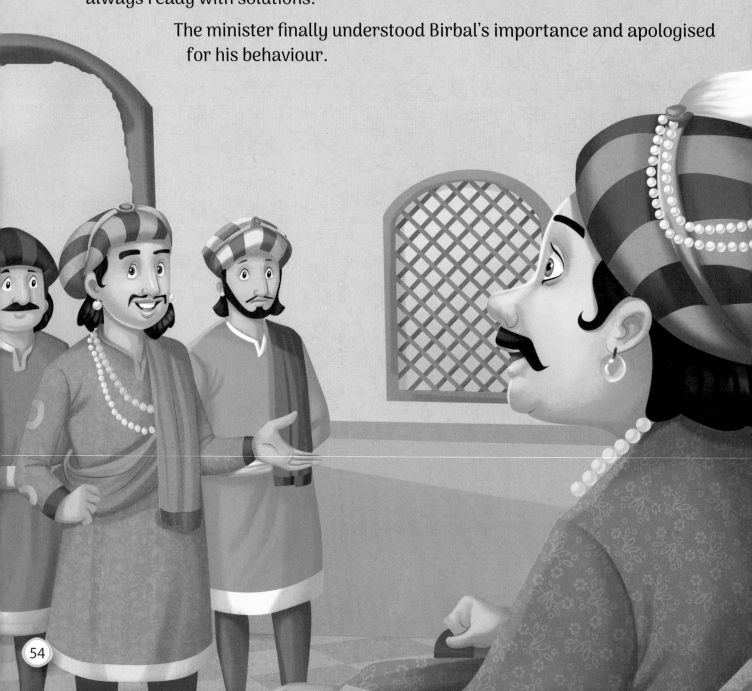

Under the Shade of Birbal's Wit

Once, Emperor Akbar was irritated after Birbal cracked a joke. He was furious and asked Birbal never to show his face in the city again. Birbal left the city and disappeared.

When Akbar's anger subsided, he realised his mistake and started missing Birbal. He knew that Birbal could not resist solving challenges. So, he announced, "I will reward anyone who can walk under sunlight and yet remain in the shade, without using an umbrella."

A few days later, a villager entered Akbar's palace holding a cot over his head. He bowed to Akbar and said, "Jahanpanah, I have come here to collect my reward."

Akbar rewarded him and said, "Now, take me to the person who gave you this idea."

Akbar and the villager went back to his village, where they found Birbal living like a farmer. Akbar apologised to Birbal and asked him to re-join the royal court.

Shortening the Line

One day, Emperor Akbar presented an unusual challenge to his ministers. He took a piece of chalk and drew a line on the floor. He then said to his ministers, "Can any of you shorten this line without touching it?"

The ministers sought some time to discuss the problem. Akbar gave them an hour to come up with the solution. All the ministers went into a huddle, but no one could come up with an answer. It seemed impossible to them.

Birbal entered the court at that moment. When the ministers told him about Akbar's challenge, he smiled and said, "I can solve it."

He took a piece of chalk and drew a line longer than the first, and said, "Huzoor, now the line you drew has become shorter!"

Akbar smiled at this simple solution, and all the ministers praised Birbal's wit.

Sense and Sight

Once, Akbar summoned his ministers and said, "The queen wishes to distribute alms to the blind. Make a list of all the blind people in my kingdom."

The ministers compiled the list and submitted it to Akbar. Akbar asked Birbal to cross-check the list.

Birbal looked at the list and said, "Jahapanah, I think we can add more people to the list. There are more blind people in our kingdom." Akbar asked Birbal to prove his statement.

The next day, Birbal went and sat under a tree, repairing a shoe. An acquaintance passing by saw Birbal and asked him, "What are you doing?"

Birbal didn't reply. He simply signalled to his assistant, who wrote down the man's name on a scroll. People kept asking him the same question all day long, and the list of names grew bigger.

Soon, one of the spies reported Birbal's actions to Akbar. He could not believe the news, so he summoned Birbal to court. Birbal came, but he sat down and started to mend shoes in the court as well.

Confused, Akbar asked, "What are you doing, Birbal?"

Birbal nodded to the assistant, and he scribbled something on the scroll. Birbal replied, "Your Majesty, I was adding more people to the list of the blind, as instructed by you."

Birbal then handed his list to the emperor. Akbar was surprised to see his name on the list. He got angry and asked, "Why is my name in your list of blind people?"

Birbal politely replied, "Huzoor, all the people on the list, including you, asked me what I was doing! Was it not clear that I was repairing shoes? Just because you can see doesn't mean you cannot be blind to things around you."

Akbar laughed loudly and agreed with Birbal's assessment.

The Blind Saint ✳

There was once a young girl named Ganga, who had not uttered a word since her parents were killed in front of her. A blind saint in Akbar's kingdom was renowned for his extraordinary healing powers. So, Ganga's uncle took her to the blind saint to cure her.

As soon as they entered the saint's chamber, Ganga pointed to the blind saint and started screaming, "Uncle! He killed my parents!"

The blind saint became furious and said, "What nonsense! I can't see anything, and this kid is accusing me of murder. Take her away from me!"

Ganga's uncle was embarrassed and took her home. Ganga kept crying and insisting that she was telling the truth. Her uncle too was perturbed as his niece had said something after so long.

Finally, he believed her story. He took Ganga to the royal court and narrated the incident to Emperor Akbar.

Akbar asked Birbal to solve the case as soon as possible. Birbal summoned the blind saint to the court. As soon as the blind saint arrived, Birbal took out his sword and charged at him without any warning. When the saint saw that Birbal was about to kill him, he picked a sword kept nearby and got ready to defend himself. He did not realise that he had fallen into Birbal's trap. Everyone was surprised upon seeing the saint's reaction.

Akbar bellowed, "He is a fraudster! Arrest this murderer and hang him tomorrow."

The soldiers arrested the saint and took him to prison. Akbar praised Ganga for her courage and gave her several gifts. He also rewarded Birbal for solving the case so quickly.

An Unlucky Face

In Akbar's kingdom, there lived a man named Yusuf. People used to believe that seeing Yusuf's face would bring them bad luck. One of Akbar's ministers told Akbar that meeting Yusuf in the morning could ruin one's day.

Akbar replied, "I don't believe in such nonsense. Bring Yusuf to my courtroom tomorrow, and I shall see his face myself. I want to dispel all such superstitious notions."

The next day, the minister presented Yusuf in Akbar's court. As soon as Akbar saw Yusuf, a messenger informed Akbar that his grandson had fallen ill. Anxious upon hearing this, Akbar rushed out of the room, and slipped and fell on the floor. By then, Akbar was sure that seeing Yusuf's face had brought him bad luck.

Akbar ordered his soldiers to lock Yusuf in prison and hang him the next morning.

Yusuf was shocked and begged for mercy. However, the guards dragged him to prison. Birbal felt sorry for poor Yusuf, who was punished wrongly. Birbal went to prison to meet him and whispered a plan in his ears.

The next morning, Yusuf insisted on meeting the emperor before he was executed. Akbar summoned him to the court and enquired, "What do you want, Yusuf?"

Yusuf replied, "Jahanpanah, you punished me because you thought my face brings misfortune to others. However, my life was ruined because I saw your face. Does this mean that your face brings greater misfortune to others?"

Akbar immediately realised his mistake of believing a silly superstition and set Yusuf free after giving him many gifts.

The Sun and the Moon ❋ ❋

Emperor Akbar often tested his ministers by asking them tricky questions or giving them puzzles to solve. Once, while taking a stroll, he asked his ministers, "We know that the Sun and Moon are high up in the sky, and are visible to all. But, I am curious to know if there is anything that they cannot see from there, which we can see."

All the ministers were stumped by the question and did not reply. Finally, Akbar looked at Birbal and asked, "Birbal, why are you not replying?"

Birbal smiled and said, "Huzoor, they cannot see darkness as they always light up our world. But we can see darkness when there is no light source present."

As always, Birbal's answer impressed Akbar. He looked at Birbal with great admiration and rewarded him for his wise reply.

❋ The Collision ❋

One day, Akbar decided to play a prank on Birbal in the royal court. He looked at his ministers and said, "I had an amusing dream last night. In my dream, it was a dark, moonless night. I was walking in a strange land and could not see anything properly. Suddenly, I collided with Birbal."

By now, Akbar's ministers were excited. They insisted that Akbar tell them what happened next. Akbar continued with a naughty smile, "There was a pool of cream nearby, and I fell into it. However, Birbal was not so lucky, and fell into a gutter."

Everyone, including Akbar, started laughing after imagining Birbal's condition in Akbar's dream. Birbal smiled and remained poised. Akbar was thrilled as he thought he had finally scored one over Birbal.

When everyone stopped laughing, Akbar looked at Birbal and teased him, "Birbal, you are unusually quiet. Don't you have anything to say about my dream yet?"

Everyone looked at Birbal, waiting for his response. Birbal calmly replied, "Huzoor, I was quiet because I was wondering how we could experience the same dream last night! But I guess you woke up early and didn't finish the dream. Luckily, I kept sleeping and saw the whole dream."

Akbar was confused and said, "Really? What did you see Birbal?"

Birbal replied, "When I came out of the gutter, and you came out of the pool of cream, we realised that we had no water to clean ourselves. So, we decided to lick each other."

Akbar turned red with embarrassment and realised that he could never outwit Birbal.

The Three Dolls

A craftsman once approached Emperor Akbar and said, "Jahanpanah! I have crafted three identical animal dolls. Can anyone in your court tell me the difference between the three dolls?"

Akbar and his ministers looked at the dolls but couldn't find any difference. However, Birbal analysed them for hours and said, "Each of these has a small hole in its ear. If you pass a wire through the hole, it comes out from the mouth of the first doll. It represents people who cannot keep a secret. The wire comes out from the ear of the second doll and represents people who don't understand anything that is said to them. However, the wire goes to the heart of the third doll and does not come out. It represents people who can keep a secret."

The craftsman bowed to Birbal and applauded his wisdom.

Neither Here nor There

❋ ❋

A minister in Akbar's court was jealous of Birbal because Akbar always praised Birbal's wit. He approached Akbar and complained, "Forgive my audacity jahanpanah, but you always assign the most important tasks to Birbal. Please give me a chance to prove my skills too."

Akbar smiled, gave three bags to the minister, and said, "Take these three bags filled with money. Spend the first bag to buy something from here. Spend the second to buy something from there; and spend the third on something that is neither here nor there."

The minister left immediately to finish the task. However, he could not solve the challenge even after two days. He returned to court and said to Akbar, "Huzoor! It is impossible to complete this task, and I doubt that even Birbal can succeed in fulfilling this challenge of yours."

Akbar then called Birbal and assigned the same task to him. The next day, Birbal came to the court and reported, "I have completed the task, Your Majesty! I spent the money in the first bag to buy sweets. Hence, I used it to buy something here. I distributed the money in the second pouch among the poor and asked them to pray to God for a better life for you in heaven, so I got something for you from there. I spent the money in the third pouch on a bet, so I spent it on something which is neither here nor there."

Everyone was amazed by how Birbal had fulfilled the task. The minister was embarrassed and accepted defeat. He admitted that Birbal deserved praise and recognition for his wit. Akbar rewarded Birbal for successfully solving the riddle.

Birbal Stops a Rumour

One day, Birbal was on his way to a spice market, when a stranger approached him and said, "I can't believe my eyes. You are Birbal! People say that you are the smartest minister in Emperor Akbar's court."

Birbal smiled at the stranger and said, "Yes, my name is Birbal."

The stranger continued, "On my way here, many people told me about your generosity. I have travelled so far just to see you in person."

Birbal realised that the man was trying to flatter him in order to ask for a favour or some money.

He firmly said to the stranger, "Please do me a favour. On your way back, tell these people that the tales about my generosity are completely false!"

Realising that he won't be able to trick Birbal, the stranger bid him farewell.

The Unreal Lion

Emperor Akbar was a close friend of the Shah of Persia. They often challenged each other by exchanging tough riddles.

One day, the Shah sent an artificial lion that was kept inside an iron cage to Akbar's court. The Shah's messenger bowed before Akbar and said, "Your Majesty! Our king has challenged you to take this lion out of its cage without opening, breaking, or modifying the cage. You have three weeks to solve this riddle."

Akbar noticed that the lion was a replica. He looked at his courtiers, hoping they would have a solution. However, none of them knew how to take such a huge lion out without touching the cage. Akbar was worried and stressed as he did not wish to accept defeat to the Shah of Persia. Fortunately, Birbal, who had been out of town and was not expected to return soon, entered the court. Akbar told him about the riddle and asked him to solve it. Birbal examined the lion carefully and realised that it was made of wax.

He said to Akbar, "Your Majesty! Please give me one day."

The next day, Birbal brought an iron rod to the court. He then heated one end of the rod until it became red hot. Finally, he passed the iron rod through the cage's bars and stuck it into the lion's mouth. Soon the wax lion started melting and turned into liquid wax. Birbal then allowed the molten wax to trickle out of the cage.

The riddle was solved. Akbar sent a messenger to the Shah of Persia with the answer. Birbal was thus rewarded for saving Akbar's reputation.

The Butcher and the Grain Merchant

There was a butcher in Emperor Akbar's kingdom. After selling meat, he put the money he earned in a pouch that was kept near the counter. The butcher was about to close the shop when a grain merchant entered and requested some fresh meat.

He quickly packed it, but meanwhile, the merchant grabbed the butcher's pouch and took out money to pay him.

The butcher roared, "What are you doing? This is my money!"

But, the merchant looked at him in surprise and said, "What are you saying? This is my pouch." Soon, both of them started fighting. Several shopkeepers assembled at the butcher's shop. Everyone suggested that they take the matter to the king's court.

Both the merchant and the butcher presented themselves before Akbar. The emperor asked Birbal for his counsel. He listened to both of them carefully and then asked the merchant to give him the pouch for examination. On a closer look, he realised that the coins inside the pouch had blood stains on them.

He asked the merchant, "During your fight, did the butcher snatch this pouch from you?" The merchant replied, "He tried to grab the pouch, but I didn't let him touch it."

At once, Birbal realised that the merchant was lying. He then announced, "The coins in the pouch have bloodstains on them. This would only be possible if the butcher had touched them and dropped them inside the pouch. Hence, the pouch belongs to the butcher."

The butcher thanked Birbal for delivering a just decision. The grain merchant was arrested by the soldiers and sent to prison.

No Hair on the Palm

One morning, when Birbal entered the court, he saw that Akbar was staring at his palm. Intrigued by Akbar's actions, Birbal asked, "What are you staring at, Jahanpanah?" Akbar replied, "Birbal, I was wondering why my palms are hairless!"

Birbal smiled and said, "It's because of your generosity. You always shower people with gifts and donate to the poor. Your hands keep rubbing against these gifts, and hence your palms are hairless."

Akbar smiled and enquired, "Then, why don't you have any hair on your palms either?"

Birbal wittily replied, "It's because I receive many gifts from you, and my hands often rub against them."

Akbar laughed aloud and gave his necklace to Birbal as a reward for his witty reply.

Birbal Retrieves the Ring

While on a hunting trip in the forest, Akbar and Birbal started feeling thirsty. Akbar spotted a well and stopped to fetch water from it. He peeped into the well but was disappointed to see that it was dry. Suddenly, one of Akbar's rings slipped from his hands and fell into the well.

He called for Birbal's help. Birbal quickly brought some fresh cow dung and threw it inside the well. It fell on the ring. He then tied a stone with a long rope and dropped it on the cow dung, and tied the other end of the rope to a large boulder. Akbar and Birbal then resumed their hunting expedition.

On their way back, they stopped by the well. Birbal pulled the rope up and retrieved the dried cow dung attached to the stone. When he flipped it, they found Akbar's ring stuck to it. Akbar thanked Birbal for retrieving his precious ring.

The Devotional Singer ❋

Tansen, a melodious singer, was one among the navratnas in Emperor Akbar's court. One day, Akbar praised him and said, "Tansen, you are the most soulful singer on this continent."

Tansen replied, "I am honoured by your praise, Jahanpanah. But my teacher, Swami Haridas, is a far superior singer."

Akbar was surprised. He said, "If your teacher is better than you, I want to hear his music. Invite him to the royal court, and I will grant him a suitable position."

Tansen replied, "Your Majesty! My teacher prefers to live in the forest and sing anonymously. He does not seek any recognition. He won't leave his ashram."

Akbar was intrigued by Tansen's reply. He decided to go to Swami Haridas' ashram to hear him sing. He was accompanied by Tansen and Birbal. Swami Haridas gave them a warm welcome. Akbar waited patiently, but Swami Haridas did not sing. Akbar was disappointed, but Birbal asked him to wait for another day. The next

morning, Akbar and Birbal were taking a stroll in the forest when they heard the melodious voice of Swami Haridas. He was singing a devotional song. Akbar closed his eyes and felt as if he had been transported to another realm. After listening to the music, Akbar said, "I wonder why Swami Haridas' voice was even more soulful than Tansen's!"

Birbal replied, "Your Majesty! It's because Swami Haridas doesn't sing for money or rewards. He intends to please God with his music. So, he sings when he wants and sings with absolute devotion."

Akbar understood the secret and nodded in agreement.

The Biggest Fool

Once, Emperor Akbar asked Birbal to make a list of all the foolish people in Agra. Birbal immediately left the court to fulfil this task.

While Birbal was away, a merchant came to Akbar's court with a beautiful horse. He said, "Your Majesty! This is one of the finest breeds of horses. It is sturdy and as quick as a thunderbolt." Akbar was impressed by the Arabian horse's beauty and charm. He said, "I like your horse. I would like to buy it." The merchant was euphoric and replied, "Your Majesty! I have a hundred more such horses. However, I couldn't bring those with me because I didn't have the money. I will need one lakh gold coins to bring them here."

Akbar gave the merchant the required sum of money and two weeks to get the horses. The merchant thanked Akbar and left.

Soon, Birbal arrived at the court. Akbar was so excited that he took Birbal to the stable and told him about the deal. Instead of congratulating Akbar, Birbal said, "You put your trust in a stranger and paid him one lakh gold coins! There is no guarantee that he will return." However, Akbar kept insisting that he was sure that the merchant would bring him the rest of the horses.

Birbal quickly added Akbar's name to his list of fools. Akbar saw this and asked Birbal why his name was there. Birbal said, "Any man who pays such a large sum in advance, and expects the merchant to actually return, has to be a fool." Akbar argued, "What if I am right, Birbal? What if the merchant returns with the horses?"

Birbal replied, "I'm sure he won't! However, if he does, I'll replace your name with his!"

Akbar laughed as he realised he couldn't win an argument with Birbal.

The Music Competition

Emperor Akbar hosted a singing competition at his court. He invited all the renowned musicians of his kingdom to take part in this competition. When everybody arrived, he presented a bull before them and announced, "Whoever can impress this bull with their music, will be the winner of this competition."

Akbar's words surprised everyone. The musicians played their best songs for the bull. However, the beast wasn't impressed. Finally, Birbal came forward with his instrument and started creating the sounds of a cow mooing and mosquitoes humming. To everyone's surprise, the bull took an interest in Birbal's music.

Akbar laughed out loud and said, "Very good, Birbal! Only you know that music has to be played according to the audience's taste. I declare you the winner of this competition."

The Greedy Eater

One summer day, Akbar invited Birbal to his chamber and served him delicious mangoes from the royal garden. Lost in their conversation, Akbar and Birbal kept eating mangoes and throwing mango seeds under their table.

Akbar saw the mango seeds and decided to play a prank on Birbal. He quietly pushed all his mango seeds towards Birbal's side and said, "Birbal, I didn't know you liked mangoes so much! Look at how many mangoes you have eaten all alone!"

Birbal looked under the table and understood Akbar's plan to tease him. He smiled and replied, "I do like mangoes, but I am not as greedy as you, huzoor. You enjoyed the mangoes so much that you swallowed the seeds along with the pulp!"

Akbar laughed heartily at Birbal's witty response.

The Magical Donkey ✳

One day, Akbar lost a ring in the royal court. He gloomily said, "Birbal, I lost my grandfather's ring in the court and cannot find it."

Birbal replied, "One of the courtiers must have found the ring and did not return it to you. Don't worry, I will catch the thief."

Birbal left the court and returned with a donkey. He announced, "This is a magical donkey. All of you must hold its tail. The donkey will reveal the truth when the thief touches its tail."

After everyone had touched the donkey's tail, Birbal asked them to show him their hands. All the courtiers had a black stain on their hands, except one.

Birbal pointed to that man and said, "I applied black paint on the donkey's tail. But he didn't hold the donkey's tail for fear of getting caught. Here's your thief!"

Akbar sent the courtier to prison and rewarded Birbal.

The Diamond Thief

A swindler named Chaman lived in Emperor Akbar's kingdom. He earned his living by deceiving and tricking people. One day, he invited a diamond merchant named Lobhichand to his house for dinner. Lobhichand gladly accepted Chaman's invitation and went to his house for dinner.

The next morning, Chaman started shouting in front of Lobhichand's house, "You thief! Come out. You stole a diamond when you came to my house last night. Return it to me at once!" Lobhichand was surprised and denied his accusations. They fought for some time and finally went to Akbar's court to settle the dispute.

Chaman addressed Akbar and said, "Jahanpanah, I have three witnesses who could testify that Lobhichand stole a diamond from my house."

Birbal asked Chaman to produce the witnesses.

The first witness was a tailor, the second a cobbler, and the third a barber. Birbal gave all the three witnesses a lump of clay and said, "Use it to sculpt the shape of Chaman's diamond."

Birbal sent them to separate rooms. The barber sculpted a razor; the tailor moulded the clay into a needle, while the cobbler carved a punch.

Birbal showed the objects to Akbar and said, "None of the three men have seen a diamond in their lives. They only know that a diamond is one of the most precious objects in the world. So, they sculpted the objects most valuable to them. Chaman is lying!"

Chaman fell at Akbar's feet and begged for forgiveness, but Akbar sent him to the royal prison. Everyone in court praised Birbal's intelligence.

Birbal Acts Like a Child

Birbal reached the court quite late one day. Akbar inquired the reason for his delay. Birbal replied, "Your Majesty! My son was crying. It was tough to console him."

Akbar retorted, "Oh, Birbal! How difficult is it to console a child? Don't give me excuses!"

Suddenly, Birbal started crying and acting like a child. When Akbar tried to calm him down, Birbal demanded, "Father, I want a cow!"

Understanding Birbal's plan, Akbar ordered his men to bring a cow. However, Birbal started crying again and said, "Father, I want milk!"

Akbar ordered his men to milk the cow and give it to Birbal. Birbal had some of the milk and started crying again. Akbar was frustrated and asked, "What do you want now?"

Birbal replied, "Now please put the milk back into the cow."

Akbar laughed and said, "I give up, Birbal! You're right. It is tough to soothe a kid."

The Fastest Horse

Birbal once reached Akbar's court looking extremely tired. When Akbar asked him the reason, Birbal said, "My wife and children have gone to meet my in-laws. They took my chariot. So, I walked to the palace."

Akbar immediately ordered the manager of his stable to send the fastest horse in the stable to Birbal. The stable manager disliked Birbal, so he sent a weak and sick horse to Birbal's house. The horse was so ill that it died the same night. Birbal had to walk to reach the royal court again the next day.

Akbar asked him, "You are now in possession of the fastest horse we have, why are you late again then?"

Birbal replied, "Your Majesty, the horse was so fast that it reached heaven in just one night."

Akbar realised the mischief of the stable manager and punished him. He gifted Birbal a new and fast horse for travelling.

The Real Master

One day, two men came to Akbar's court arguing with each other. The first man said, "I am a merchant, and I had to travel to a different kingdom to expand my business. This man is my servant. I trusted him with my house in my absence. However, he stole my money and is now claiming that he is the real owner of my house."

The second man protested, "He's an imposter, Jahanpanah! I am the real owner of the house, and he's trying to steal it from me."

Perplexed, Akbar asked Birbal to intervene. Birbal sternly said, "I can read minds and I know who is lying."

He then looked at the guard and thundered, "Execute the servant!"

The guard was confused, but he still took out his sword and moved forward. Fearing that he had been discovered, the second man fell upon Akbar's feet and started begging for mercy.

Akbar sent the servant to prison and praised Birbal's intelligence.

The Red Hot Test

One day, a man approached Emperor Akbar and said, "Your Majesty! This man, Hasan, has stolen my wife's necklace. Ask him to hold a hot iron rod in his hand. If he's honest, the deities won't let his hand burn."

Akbar agreed and ordered Hasan to take the test the next day. Worried, Hasan went to Birbal's house and asked for his help. Birbal came up with a plan. The next day, Hasan appeared in the court and said, "I insist that the rich man take the test first, since he is the one accusing me of this crime. If he isn't lying, the red hot iron rod won't hurt him either."

The rich man panicked and suggested that he might be mistaken. Akbar realised that the rich man was lying. As a punishment, he asked him to give the necklace to Hasan.

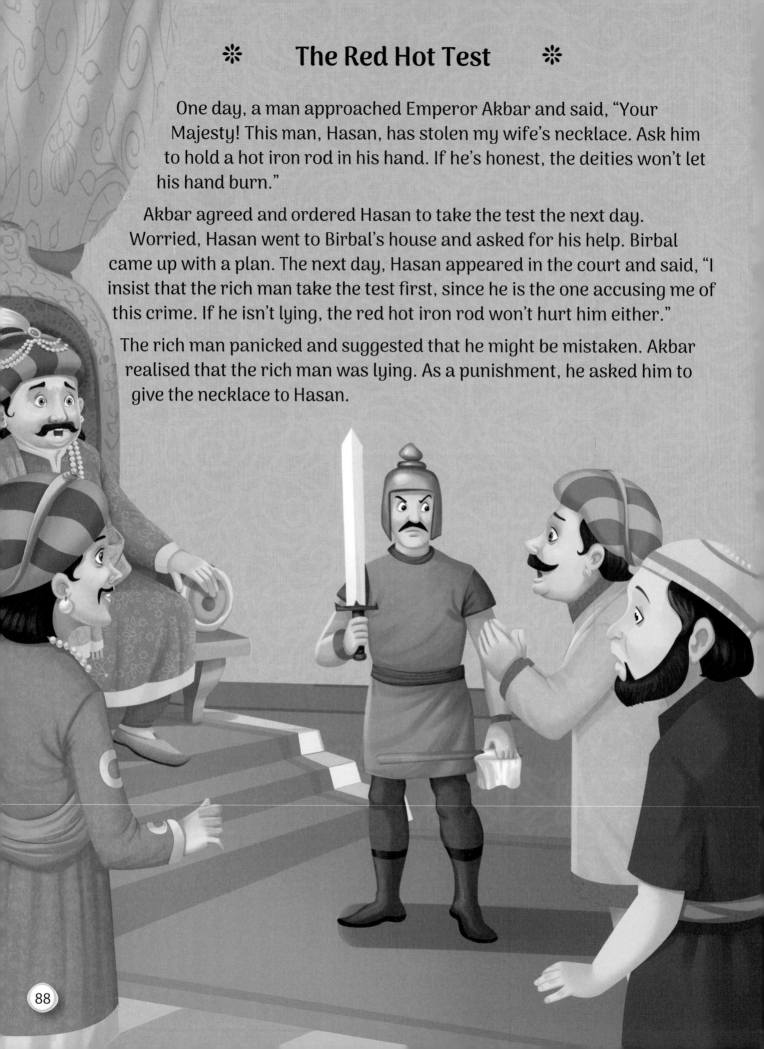

The Devotion of God

One day, Emperor Akbar asked Birbal, "Why does God always come to rescue his devotees himself? Why can't he send his servants?"

Birbal asked for some time to answer Akbar's question. In the meantime, he got a wax statue of Akbar's grandson created. He then asked the prince's caretaker to take it to the lake and wait for his signal. When Birbal and Akbar came to the lake, Birbal nodded to the caretaker. She dropped the statue into the lake.

Not knowing about Birbal's ploy, Akbar immediately jumped into the lake to save his grandson, but soon realised that it was a mere statue.

Birbal then asked Akbar, "Huzoor, you have many servants at your service. Why did you jump into the lake yourself?"

Akbar replied, "I love my grandson! I wanted to personally ensure his safety."

Birbal smiled and said, "God loves his devotees too, and hence He always comes to their rescue."

A List of Four Fools

Emperor Akbar once asked Birbal to make a list of four of the greatest fools in his kingdom. Birbal immediately left the court to fulfil his task. On his way, he saw a man who was riding a horse, while carrying wooden logs on his own head, as he didn't want to overload his horse. Next, he met a man who had raised his hands in the air to remember the correct dimensions of a vessel, rather than carrying the vessel to the market. He presented both the fools in the court.

But Akbar was not happy and complained, "Birbal, I asked you to find four of the greatest fools. However, you brought only two."

Birbal replied, "Your Majesty, The third fool is you, for assigning such a stupid task; and the fourth is me, for doing this task."

Akbar couldn't control his laughter upon hearing Birbal's witty response.

The Miraculous Saint

One day, Akbar was offended by a joke Birbal cracked. He roared, "Birbal! Get out of my court! I banish you from my city and kingdom. If I see you again, I shall have you executed."

Following Akbar's orders, Birbal immediately left the court. Several weeks went by, and Akbar started missing Birbal. He sent his spies in all directions but could not find him. Soon, a holy saint, along with his two disciples, arrived at Akbar's court. The disciples claimed that their teacher was a great scholar and could perform all sorts of miracles. Akbar was intrigued by this saint. He asked his courtiers to ask the saint the most challenging questions to check his brilliance. All of the Akbar's courtiers started posing difficult questions to the saint. To everybody's surprise, the saint answered each one of those accurately.

Akbar was impressed with the saint's replies, and finally, it was his turn to ask a question. He said, "Can you tell me who is the greatest enemy of an emperor?"

The saint replied, "It's his poor sense of humor."

Akbar asked several more questions, and the saint answered all of them to his satisfaction. Finally, Akbar said, "I hear you can also perform miracles. Can you present my ex-minister Birbal before me?"

The saint replied, "Of course, I can!"

Saying this, the saint started to remove his beard and the wig from his head. Within no time, the saint had transformed into Birbal. Akbar's eyes brightened to see his dear minister. Akbar immediately hugged Birbal and asked him to rejoin the royal court. Birbal thanked Akbar and resumed his duties as a minister.

The Elephant's Footprint

Emperor Akbar loved his queen dearly. When she asked him to make her brother the diwan of his kingdom, he couldn't refuse. Akbar asked Birbal to step down from the post and announced that his brother-in-law was the new diwan. One day, Akbar and his new diwan were travelling when Akbar noticed the footprints of his elephant and thought of a plan to test his brother-in-law's intelligence.

He said, "I want you to guard this footprint for three days."

The new diwan was surprised to receive such a request, but he agreed to follow Akbar's orders. He spent three days and nights around the footprint and informed Akbar of his success on the fourth day. Akbar was now sure that his brother-in-law wasn't suited for the job of the diwan. Akbar then called Birbal and assigned the same task to him. Birbal erected an iron poll near the footprint and tied a fifty-meter-long rope to the pole. He then announced, "By the emperor's orders, we need to protect this footprint.

Hence, we'll be demolishing all the houses that lie within a fifty-meter radius of this footprint."

The villagers panicked and offered to protect the footprint day and night. Birbal then said, "Alright! We will not destroy the houses, if you agree to protect this footprint."

The villagers agreed and erected a fence around the footprint. Birbal then said, "I shall be back after three days."

Birbal went back to the royal court and explained to Akbar how he had managed to ensure that the footprint would remain untouched. Akbar said to his brother-in-law, "Birbal has accomplished the task faster and more efficiently with his innovative approach. You are not fit for this job."

Akbar then re-appointed Birbal as his diwan.

Akbar and the Saint

Years of his reign had made Akbar a little arrogant as his courtiers always tried to flatter him and agreed with everything he said.

One day, Akbar was strolling in his royal garden when he bumped into a saint, who was lying on the ground. Akbar was furious and said, "How dare you enter my garden? Get up at once!"

The saint turned around and asked, "Oh! So, is this your garden?"

Akbar replied, "Of course, it is! This garden, its roses, their fragrance, the river, its water, this palace, this city, and even this kingdom belongs to me."

The saint questioned him again, "But I wonder, who was its owner before your birth?"

Akbar replied patiently, "Before me, all these things belonged to my father, and before him, they belonged to my grandfather."

The saint became excited and said, "I got it! It means, one day, all of this will belong to your child and then your grandchild."

Akbar was intrigued by the behaviour of the saint and replied, "Yes, indeed!"

The saint then asked, "So, basically, you are like a custodian, just like the innkeeper of an inn. Isn't this world like an inn, and people are mere travelers who stay in it? You come to this world and somethings belong to you, but when you leave, the same things belong to someone else. This means that nothing is ours. Everything remains here."

Akbar's replied, "I am impressed with your philosophy. Who are you?"

The saint removed his beard and wig. Akbar was surprised to see Birbal standing in front of him. He said with excitement, "I loved our discussion, Birbal. Let's go inside and discuss more philosophy."

The Bag of Gold

An old woman once decided to embark on a pilgrimage. She had a few gold coins as her savings. She kept the gold coins inside a small pouch and sewed the pouch. She then went to a respected judge and said, "Sir, I am going on a pilgrimage. Please take care of my bag. I shall collect the bag from you after I return."

The judge agreed to keep the bag safe until the old woman returned. A few months later, the woman returned, and the judge returned the pouch to her. The woman cut the stitches on the bag and looked inside. She was shocked to see a few pebbles inside the pouch. The woman accused the judge of stealing her money.

The judge harshly replied, "I did not open yourt bag. I am a wealthy man, and I don't need your money. Stop lying, or I will throw you inside a prison."

The woman was devastated after losing her entire savings. She went to the royal court and after narrating the entire incident, she pleaded to Akbar, "Jahanpanah, please give me justice. The judge should be punished for his actions."

The judge was an influential person, and Akbar did not want to punish him without any proof. He asked Birbal to investigate the matter further. Birbal examined the pouch and asked the woman, "Did you notice any tampering in the stitches on the bag when the judge gave it back to you?"

The woman replied, "No."

Birbal asked the lady to come back after two days. Later in the day, Birbal said to Akbar, "Huzoor, before going to sleep tonight, please cut your bedsheet into two."

Akbar was intrigued, but he agreed to Birbal's plan. He cut one of the sheets into two and went to sleep.

By noon next day, Akbar was surprised to see that the torn bedsheet had been sewn together so perfectly that he could not find any cut marks. Akbar told Birbal about the incident. Birbal summoned the servants and asked them about the person who had sewn the bedsheet.

The servants took Birbal to a tailor's shop. Birbal showed the old woman's bag to the tailor there and asked him, "Do you remember this bag?"

The tailor replied, "Yes. A few weeks ago, a judge from our town came to me. He asked me to remove the stitches on the bag. After removing gold coins from the bag, he placed pebbles inside and asked me to stitch it up again."

Birbal reported the matter to the king. Akbar summoned the judge and asked him to return the gold coins to the old woman. Later, the judge was removed from his post and thrown inside a prison.

The Milk of an Ox

One day, Birbal was late in reaching the royal court. One of the ministers complained, "Jahanpanah is always lenient with Birbal and relies on him unnecessarily."

Akbar did not want to seem partial and replied, "Birbal is resourceful and accomplishes any task I give him, that is why I rely on him."

The minister replied, "If he is so resourceful, please ask Birbal to fetch the milk of an ox."
Insistent on proving his impartiality, Akbar agreed to do so.

When Birbal came to the court, Akbar ordered Birbal to bring him the milk of an ox. Birbal protested, saying that it was impossible, but Akbar was adamant. Akbar said, "Don't come back to the court until you can bring me the milk of an ox." Birbal bowed and left.

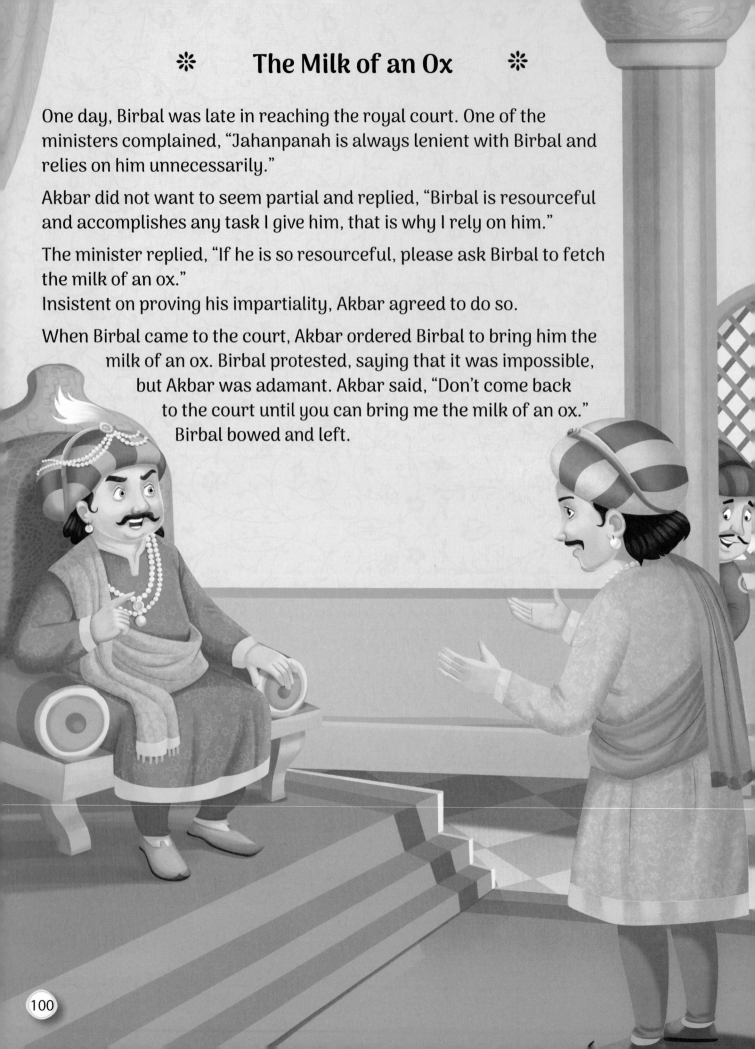

A few weeks later, Akbar was walking near a lake, early in the morning, when he saw Birbal's daughter washing clothes in the lake. Akbar approached the girl and asked, "Why are you washing clothes so early in the morning?"

Birbal's daughter replied, "I don't have much time during the day. My father has given birth to a boy. I have to go back home and take care of the baby."

Akbar was furious and shouted, "Is this a joke? How can a man give birth to a baby? It's against the laws of nature."

The girl innocently replied, "Huzoor, can an ox give milk according to the laws of nature?"

Akbar was speechless after hearing her witty retort. Remorseful, Akbar asked Birbal to resume his duties.

The Most Powerful Weapon

Once upon a time, Akbar posed a question before his ministers, "What do you think is the most powerful weapon?"

While some ministers were in favour of swords, the others argued that a bow and arrow were the best.

Akbar turned towards Birbal and said, "What is your opinion?"

Birbal replied, "Jahanpanah, in my opinion, wit is the most powerful weapon. It saves us from danger. We cannot be victorious if we fight with swords, spears or bows alone."

Akbar said to his ministers, "Birbal has made an excellent point, let us test what he says."

Birbal was taking a stroll on the streets one day. He was unarmed. Akbar ordered his servants to release a mad elephant on the street. The elephant charged at Birbal. Birbal did not panic and spotted a dog near him. When the elephant came closer, Birbal threw the dog at the elephant. The dog barked at the elephant and clung on to its trunk. The elephant was scared and struggled to get rid of the dog. This gave Birbal some time to rush to safety.

Akbar was watching Birbal's actions from a distance. He was pleased to see Birbal's presence of mind and bravery. The next day, Akbar narrated the incident in the royal court and announced, "Birbal was right. Wit is indeed the most powerful weapon."

A Journey Around Earth

One day, a famous scholar came to the royal court and spoke at length about the solar system and the shape of Earth.

After the scholar stopped talking, Akbar asked him a question, "Since Earth is round, if I start moving in one direction, will I eventually return to where I had started from?"

The scholar replied, "It is possible. But to complete the journey, one needs to cross oceans, mountains and forests. Though you can sail through oceans and build tunnels, it may still take very long to complete the trip." Akbar then asked his ministers, "Tell me, how many years would it take to complete the journey?"

One of the ministers speculated, "It will take 25 years, Jahapanah."

Akbar then asked Birbal, "Why are you silent? Don't you have an answer?"

Birbal smiled and replied, "Jahanpanah, it will take just one day to complete this journey, but only if you travel at the speed of the Sun!"

Akbar applauded Birbal's witty answer. He also rewarded the scholar for sharing his knowledge with the members of the royal court.

A Hasty Verdict

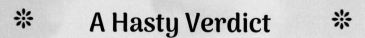

Once, King Akbar and Birbal were walking in a mango orchard, when suddenly, an arrow landed near Akbar's feet. Akbar ordered his guards to catch the archer. The young archer was trembling with fear when the guards arrested him. King Akbar came up to the boy and demanded, "Who has sent you to kill me?"

The boy meekly replied, "I was not trying to kill you. I was only trying to knock down a mango. I missed and the arrow flew in your direction. Please forgive me!"

Birbal pleaded on behalf of the boy, but Akbar was angry and refused to forgive him.

"Kill the boy in the same manner as he tried to kill me," ordered Akbar.

The guards tied the boy to a mango tree. As they were aiming to shoot the arrow, Birbal rushed forward and shouted, "Stop! Don't shoot! Did you pay attention to our king's order? To fulfil his command, you must aim for a mango. The arrow must miss the mango and then strike the boy."

The guards looked towards Akbar, waiting for further instructions. Akbar realised that he had made a hasty judgement and was punishing the boy for an act he did not commit intentionally. He said to the guards, "Set the boy free. It was an accident."

The boy thanked Birbal for saving his life and promised to be more careful in the future.

Akbar and the Shawl

The senior ministers in Akbar's court were jealous of Birbal because Akbar valued Birbal's advice highly. One day, they went to Akbar and complained, "Your Majesty, you favour Birbal more, even though he is junior to us. We request you to give us one chance to prove that we are better than Birbal."

King Akbar thought for a moment and said, "I'm not partial towards Birbal, so I accept your request."

Akbar gave them a shawl and said, "I want you to cover my whole body with this." All the ministers tried their best to cover Akbar's body with the shawl. However, it was too small, and they were unable to complete the challenge.

Finally, the ministers accepted defeat.

Akbar then summoned Birbal and presented the same challenge to him. Birbal asked Akbar to lie down on a bed. He then smiled and said, "Huzoor, I request you to bend your knees and curl up your body."

Akbar curled up his body, and Birbal successfully covered it with a shawl.

King Akbar rewarded Birbal and told his ministers, "I have proved to you that I hold Birbal in high esteem due to his wit and wisdom."

The ministers apologised and went back home disappointed.

❋   Four Fingers   ❋

One day, Akbar gave his ministers a riddle, "Tell me the difference between truth and falsehood in three words or less."

The courtiers couldn't think of an answer and remained quiet. Finally, Birbal answered, "Huzoor, the answer is four fingers." Akbar asked Birbal to explain his answer.

Birbal elaborated, "What we see with our own eyes is the absolute truth and can be trusted. However, we cannot trust what we hear because it can be a lie or a rumour."

Akbar nodded and said, "I agree with your assessment, but explain what you meant when you said four fingers."

"Majesty, the distance between one's eyes and ears is the width of four fingers," replied Birbal.

Akbar applauded Birbal's wise answer.

The Ill-effects of Wine

Once, King Akbar missed court for several days. Birbal was worried and went to meet Akbar in his private chamber. However, Akbar was not there. Birbal saw several wine bottles lying in the room and understood the reason behind Akbar's absence from the royal court. He hid a bottle in his shawl and went out, bumping into Akbar in the hallway. Akbar was surprised and asked, "Birbal, what are you hiding?"

Birbal blurted out, "Huzoor, it's a parrot, no, a horse... No, an elephant. Sorry, it's a donkey!" Furious, Akbar demanded an explanation.

Birbal said, "After drinking wine, a person talks like a parrot, behaves like a horse, and walks like an elephant. Eventually, the wine forces the man to act like a donkey."

Akbar realised his foolishness and decided to quit drinking.

The Worth of a Copper Coin

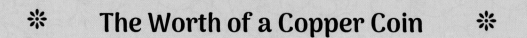

One day, a minister dropped a copper coin in Akbar's court. Birbal kneeled down and began searching for the coin. Just then, a jealous minister complained to Akbar and said, "Huzoor, look at Birbal's greed! You shower him with so many expensive gifts, yet he seeks a copper coin so desperately."

Akbar was disappointed with Birbal's behaviour and asked him to explain his actions.

Birbal picked up the coin, showed it to Akbar and said, "Jahanpanah, the coin is valuable because it has your face engraved on it. I picked it up because I did not want anyone to step on the coin accidentally. It would have been an insult to you."

Akbar was pleased to hear Birbal's response and gave him a diamond ring.

The Oily Coins ❋

One day, an oil merchant and a crook came to the court due to a dispute. The merchant complained, "This man came to my shop to buy oil. After he left, I noticed that my money was gone."

The crook protested saying that he was innocent and had never visited the oil shop. Akbar asked Birbal to settle the dispute. Birbal fetched a bowl of water. He then took out the coins from the bag and dropped them in the bowl. Soon, some oil began to float on top of the water.

Birbal announced, "The bag belongs to the oil merchant. There was a layer of oil on the coins in the bag, meaning that the merchant had touched the coins."

Akbar appreciated Birbal's wit and ordered his soldiers to throw the crook in prison.

Birbal's Painting

Once, Akbar summoned Birbal and said, "I want you to use your imagination and draw a painting for me."

Birbal protested, "Jahanpanah, I am sorry, but I cannot fulfil your command. I don't have the skills required to paint." Akbar scolded Birbal, "How dare you disobey my order? Don't come back till you finish the painting!"

A week later, Birbal returned to the court holding his creation. Akbar was shocked upon seeing the bare painting. So, Birbal explained, "Use your imagination, Your Majesty. I've painted a cow eating grass. The cow ate the grass and fled!"

Akbar laughed at Birbal's reply and praised him for his creativity.

The Half-brother

King Akbar was brought up by a nanny. The nanny had a son and Akbar treated him as his half-brother. Akbar gave his half-brother many gifts and skipped the royal court whenever he came to the royal palace. One day, King Akbar asked Birbal if he too had a half-brother or sister.

Birbal replied, "Yes, Your Majesty, I have a half-sister."

Akbar asked Birbal to bring his sister to the court. But to his surprise, Birbal arrived with a young cow. Birbal looked at Akbar and said, "Your Majesty, I have been fed cow's milk since I was a baby. The cow is like a mother to me. So, her calf is my half-sister. Perhaps I should spend more time with her too."

King Akbar laughed loudly and understood Birbal's message. After that day, he never ignored his royal duties to spend time with his half-brother again.

The Whitest One

One day, Akbar asked his ministers, "Which is the whitest thing in this world?"

Some ministers said it was cotton, while others argued that it was milk.

Finally, Birbal said, "Your Majesty, sunlight is the whitest thing in this world. Give me one day to prove my point."

Akbar agreed.

The next day, Birbal quietly put a bowl of milk and some cotton on the floor in the king's bedroom.

It was dark when Akbar got up. When he got out of bed, he accidentally spilt milk on the floor. Birbal then came in and opened the windows, and sunlight illuminated the room. He said, "Huzoor, I have proved my point. You could see the milk and the cotton only in the presence of sunlight, hence sunlight is the whitest of them all."

Akbar praised Birbal's common sense and gave him a ring as a reward.

One Question

One day, a scholar came to King Akbar's court and challenged Birbal to answer his questions. Birbal accepted the challenge. The scholar proudly asked, "Will you choose to answer a hundred easy questions, or just one difficult question?"

Birbal calmly replied, "We have spent a long day in court. I would prefer to answer one difficult question and go home."

"What came into the world first, was it the chicken, or was it the egg?" the scholar asked.

Birbal confidently answered, "The chicken." The scholar smiled, thinking he had tricked Birbal. He then asked, "Can you prove it?"

Birbal smiled and replied, "As per our agreement, you could ask only one question. I have already given you an answer. You can't ask me another question."

The scholar was left speechless.

The Other Guest

A rich man once invited Birbal to his house for lunch. When Birbal went to the man's house, he saw a hall full of people wearing identical dresses. The host greeted Birbal and said, "Only one of them is a guest. The rest are my servants. Can you find the real guest?"

Birbal accepted the challenge. Meanwhile, the host narrated several jokes to the people who had gathered in his house. Suddenly, Birbal pointed to a man and said, "He is your guest."

The host was amazed and exclaimed, "Yes! He is! How did you know?"

Birbal replied, "Your jokes were lame, but all your servants laughed, perhaps in order to appease you. Only the guest did not laugh, and looked rather annoyed. I immediately knew that he was your other guest."

The host praised Birbal, and they enjoyed a delicious feast.

✳ The Gift ✳

On the eve of Eid, Emperor Akbar summoned his ministers to a room filled with expensive gifts. He announced, "Tomorrow is a holiday, so before you leave, please pick a gift."

All the courtiers rushed forward to pick their gifts, except Birbal. After all the courtiers had left, Birbal saw that there was only a silver plate left on the table. He covered it with a cloth.

Akbar was curious and asked, "Why are you covering the plate with a cloth?" Birbal replied, "Jahapanah, if people see me carrying an empty plate, they will think that your riches are dwindling."

Akbar asked an attendant to bring a priceless statue, put it on the silver plate and said, "There is no need to hide your gift anymore." And so Birbal managed to get the most priceless gift of all.

Human Creation versus Nature

One day, Akbar was walking in the royal garden along with Birbal. He was enjoying the beauty of the garden when he saw a bunch of beautiful lilies in full bloom. Akbar pointed at the flowers and said, "Birbal, look at these beautiful flowers. Don't you think that nature's creations are the best and cannot be replicated?"

Birbal replied, "Huzoor, I agree that nature provides us with several beautiful creations. However, I believe that man can also build exquisite objects."

At that moment, the gardener's son approached them and offered Akbar a beautiful rose. Akbar thanked the boy for the gift and gave him a few gold coins as a reward.

Akbar pointed to the rose and said, "Birbal, I give you a week to prove your point. Find me an object created by man that can match the beauty of this rose."

Birbal accepted the challenge. He went to a sculptor who was famous for creating sculptures that looked real. Birbal told him about Akbar's challenge and requested him to build a bouquet that looked real. Three days later, the sculptor came to the royal court and presented a bouquet to Akbar. The sculpture was made of marble.

Akbar praised the sculptor for his creation and rewarded him handsomely. Birbal smiled and said, "Jahanpanah, I have proved my point. The sculptor's creation matches, if not surpasses, the beauty of the rose given to you by the boy. You even rewarded the sculptor more than the boy!"

Akbar agreed with Birbal and rewarded him suitably too.

The Rooster and the Hens

Akbar once wanted to play a prank on Birbal. He gave an egg to all his ministers before Birbal arrived at the royal court and asked them to hide it. The ministers hid their eggs inside their clothes. When Birbal came to the court, Akbar said, "I saw a strange dream last night. I saw a prophet who told me that I should give a test to all my ministers to fetch an egg from the royal garden. He told me that only the honest ones will find an egg there, and any dishonest ministers will have to return empty-handed."

Akbar then asked his ministers to go to the royal garden and fetch an egg. The ministers realised that Akbar was playing a prank on Birbal. They quietly went to the royal garden and acted as if they were trying to find an egg.

One by one, they all shouted, "I found an egg!"

They held up the egg that Akbar had given them and returned to the royal court.

Birbal searched the entire garden but did not find any eggs. He even jumped into a pond near the royal garden but still failed to spot any eggs. He realised that King Akbar was playing a prank. So, he came up with a plan. He entered the court acting and crowing like a rooster.

Akbar was irritated with this behaviour and sternly said, "Stop crowing! Did you get the egg?"

Birbal replied, "Jahapanah, only hens lay eggs. But I am a rooster, so I could not produce an egg."

Akbar burst out laughing and realised that it was not easy to trick his smart minister.

Mulla Do Pyaza's Head

One day, Akbar was furious with Mulla Do Pyaza. He said to his soldiers, "Behead Mulla Do Pyaza and bring me his head."

Mulla Do Pyaza was terrified when he heard about Akbar's order. He rushed to Birbal's house and fell at his feet. He pleaded to Birbal, "You are the only one who can protect me from the wrath of the emperor. I beg you to protect my life."

Birbal calmed Mulla Do Pyaza down. He then revealed his plan and said, "Do this correctly, and our emperor will definitely forgive you."

Mulla Do Pyaza thanked Birbal and went back home relieved. When the soldiers came to behead Mulla Do Pyaza, he asked them to present him before the emperor first. The soldiers agreed.

The soldiers presented Mulla Do Pyaza in the royal court. Akbar was furious with the soldiers. He shouted, "Why did you bring him here alive? I had asked you to present his head to me!"

Before the soldiers could reply, Mulla Do Pyaza politely said, "Jahanpanah, it's not their fault. I persuaded them to present me before you. I feared that they might not be able to carry out your instructions properly. Hence, I decided to present my head to you in person by carrying it on my shoulders. I also beg forgiveness for my actions."

Akbar was impressed with Mulla Do Pyaza's humble and witty reply. He forgave Mulla Do Pyaza and asked him to resume his duties. Mulla Do Pyaza profusely thanked Birbal for saving his life.

A Heavy Burden

Akbar was once travelling through his kingdom, when he saw an old mansion in ruins. Akbar said to his ministers, "I would like to build a beautiful palace at this spot. Destroy that old mansion and shift the owners to a new place."

The house belonged to an old woman. She came to Birbal's house to ask for his help. She told him, "The emperor wants to demolish my house to build a palace. It is my ancestral home, and I have several fond memories of the place. Please convince him to spare my house."

Birbal understood the woman's pain and agreed to help her. Soon, Birbal and Akbar visited the site.

They saw many empty gunny bags lying on the ground. Birbal began to load the bags with mud. Akbar curiously asked, "What are you doing, Birbal?"

Birbal replied, "I am doing this to get merit in my next life."

Akbar was intrigued and started doing the same. After filling the bags with mud, Birbal asked Akbar to help him lift the bags. Akbar tried to lift the bags but realised that they were extremely heavy.

"I'm sorry, Birbal, but they are too heavy for me!"

Birbal politely replied, "Huzoor, you say that this bag of mud is heavy. But don't you think that it is nothing when compared to the burden that snatching a poor woman's ancestral home will place on your conscience?"

Akbar realised his mistake and stopped the demolition. The poor old woman thanked Birbal for saving her house.

Shooting the Messenger

Once, a king gifted a unique parrot to Emperor Akbar. Akbar loved the parrot because the parrot could talk like humans and replied to him. Akbar kept the parrot under special security. He warned the soldiers guarding the creature, "Guard him carefully. Anyone who comes to me with the news of the parrot's death shall be executed."

The parrot passed away one day. The soldiers were too scared to report the beloved parrot's death to the king. A soldier went to Birbal and begged him to protect them from Akbar's wrath. Birbal reassured the soldier and went to meet Akbar. He bowed before the king and said, "Jahanpanah, I have come here to talk to you about your parrot."

Akbar anxiously asked, "What happened to my parrot?"

Birbal paused for a moment and stuttered, "Your parrot…"

Akbar spoke sternly, "I am asking you again! What happened to my parrot?"

Birbal replied, "Jahanpanah, your parrot neither eats anything, nor drinks water. It is neither flapping its wings, nor is it opening its eyes. It is not speaking…"

Akbar impatiently said, "Are you saying that my parrot is dead?"

Birbal bowed and said, "I did not say it, huzoor. You said it."

Akbar realised the reason behind Birbal's odd behaviour. He spared the lives of the soldiers and asked them to bury the parrot with honour. He praised Birbal for his unique way of informing him about the parrot's death.

A Hasty Reward

One day, Birbal and his friend were crossing a stream using a narrow and slippery tree trunk as a bridge. Birbal managed to cross the bridge, but his friend slipped and fell into the water. Birbal immediately threw him a rope and started to pull him out.

Birbal's friend felt grateful and hastily announced, "I'll give you twenty gold coins for saving my life!"

Suddenly, Birbal let the rope go slack. As a result, Birbal's friend fell back into the water. He shouted at Birbal, "Why did you drop me back into the stream?"

Birbal calmly replied, "Friends don't help each other in order to get rewards! Please don't ever say such a thing again." Having taught his friend a lesson, Birbal began to pull the rope again and rescued his friend successfully. Birbal's friend realised his mistake and thanked Birbal for saving his life.

Birbal Creates a Shortcut

Once, Akbar was travelling to Azabgarh. The scorching heat was making him restless, and so he asked his courtiers, "Can anyone shorten this journey for me?"

Birbal replied, "I can do it, huzoor! But you must hear a story first."

Akbar was excited and asked Birbal to narrate his story. The story was engaging, and Akbar paid full attention. When the story ended, everybody realised that they had reached Azabgarh Fort.

The other courtiers complained that they hadn't in fact taken a short cut, and had travelled the same path as usual. Birbal explained, "Huzoor, we might not have taken another path, but you did not realise the distance of the journey because you were engrossed in my story. So, I did shorten your journey."

Akbar laughed and rewarded Birbal for his enthralling storytelling.

Akbar's Dream

One night, Emperor Akbar had a strange dream. He saw that he had lost all his teeth except one. The dream perturbed Akbar, and he summoned several astrologers. He asked them the significance of such a dream. All of them gave him the same reply, "Jahapanah! Your dream means that all your relatives will die before you do."

Hearing the meaning of his dream disturbed Akbar even more. He sent away all the astrologers without giving them any rewards.

When Akbar shared his concern with Birbal, he said, "Jahanpanah, The dream also means that you'll have a longer and more prosperous life than any of your relatives!"

Birbal's positive interpretation of the dream immediately brightened Akbar's mood, and he showered Birbal with rewards.

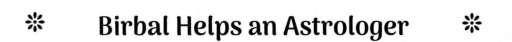

Birbal Helps an Astrologer

A smart astrologer lived in Emperor Akbar's kingdom. He always bragged about the accuracy of his predictions. One of the ministers at the royal court informed Akbar about the astrologer, so the emperor decided to test him.

After summoning the astrologer, Akbar asked him, "I have heard wonderful things about you. I want you to make one prediction for me. Tell me when you will die."

The astrologer was stumped because he knew that there was no way he could give the correct answer to this question. And King Akbar could always prove him wrong by threatening to kill him. However, he regained his composure and replied, "Jahanpanah, I need to consult my chart before I can answer that question."

Akbar said, "I give you one day. If you can answer the question correctly, you shall be rewarded handsomely."

Instead of going back to his house, the astrologer rushed to Birbal's home and narrated the entire incident. Birbal smiled and suggested a plan to the astrologer. The next day, the astrologer went to Akbar's court and said, "Jahanpanah, I can answer your question but I wish to speak to you privately."

Emperor Akbar was intrigued by the astrologer's request and agreed to speak to him in his private chamber. Once they were seated inside, the astrologer said with a grim face, "Huzoor, I will die exactly five days before your death."

Emperor Akbar realised that the astrologer was bluffing, but he did not wish to tempt fate. He gifted the astrologer several precious gems and sent him away. The astrologer thanked Birbal for saving his life and promised never again to brag about his predictions.

A Camel's Neck

Emperor Akbar was a great admirer of Birbal's wit and intellect. One day, he promised to reward Birbal with expensive gifts, but forgot all about it later. Several weeks passed, but Akbar didn't fulfil his promise. This disappointed Birbal.

A few days later, Akbar and Birbal were visiting the neighbouring kingdom, when they spotted two exotic camels. Akbar questioned Birbal, "Do you know why camels have a crooked neck?"

Birbal replied, "Your Majesty! I have heard that those who don't keep their promises are cursed with a crooked neck in their next lifetime. The same might be the case with camels."

Akbar instantly remembered his promise to Birbal. As soon as they returned to their kingdom, he sent all the promised gifts to Birbal's house. Birbal was proud as he had used his wit to get what he wanted, without actually asking for it.

A Tale of Opposites

One day, Emperor Akbar called Birbal and said, "My dear Birbal! I have a challenge for you. I want you to bring me two beings. One of them should be extremely loyal and grateful. However, the other should be the exact opposite of the first one."

All of Akbar's courtiers were sure that Birbal would lose this challenge and smugly smiled upon seeing him in an uncomfortable position. However, the very next day, Birbal arrived in court along with a dog and a young man.

He addressed Akbar saying, "Your Majesty! Next to me is my dog. He is always loyal and extremely grateful. Then, there's my brother-in-law, who's ungrateful and who always keeps complaining, despite all the good deeds I do for him! There you go, they are exact opposites."

Emperor Akbar laughed out loud and applauded Birbal for winning the challenge.

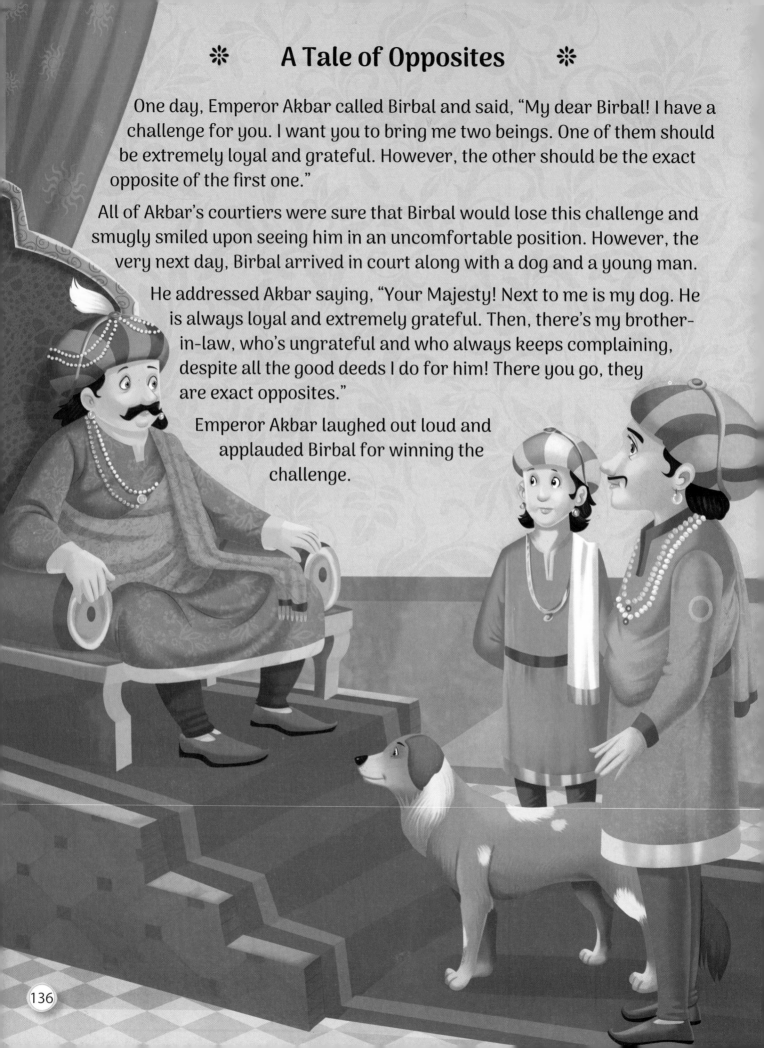

The Owl's Loan

Emperor Akbar was a passionate hunter. On one such hunting trip, Birbal was riding alongside Akbar in a forest. Suddenly, two owls hooted in a shrill voice.

Akbar noticed the owls sitting on a tree branch and asked Birbal, "Birbal! Do you know what these owls are talking about?"

Birbal replied, "I know, Your Majesty! The owls are fighting about a loan."

Akbar was surprised and asked Birbal to explain his statement.

Birbal explained, "Your Majesty! The first owl had given a loan to the second one. The creditor owl is adamant that, in repayment, he wants forty jungles that are devoid of other animals, so that he alone can rule. However, the poor owl is expressing his helplessness and saying that he can't give him such jungles."

Akbar was shocked to hear this.

Soon, the second owl hooted again, and Akbar asked Birbal to explain what it was saying this time. Birbal said, "Your Majesty! Now, the poor owl is reassuring the creditor owl that within the next few years, he will be able to repay the loan with forty empty jungles."

Akbar was curious to know how the owl would keep his promise, so he asked Birbal to explain further. Birbal replied, "The poor owl said that if the emperor kept hunting like this, soon all the jungles would be free from animals, and then there will be no problem in giving forty jungles."

Akbar immediately realised the impact of his hobby on the environment and stopped hunting from that day onwards. Birbal succeeded in saving the lives of many innocent animals.

A wealthy merchant, Ghanshyam, was famous for his miserly nature. He often made extravagant promises to people but never fulfilled any of them. He never helped the needy, nor did he treat the poor with empathy.

One day, a famous poet named Raidas visited him. Ghanshyam was fond of poetry, and so, he welcomed Raidas into his house.

Raidas recited several poems for him. Ghanshyam thoroughly enjoyed the recital and promised to reward Raidas with expensive gifts the next day.

But, the next day, the merchant mistreated Raidas and refused to reward him in any way. He shouted, "I lied to you so that I could listen to all your poems, without shelling out a penny. However, I never intended to reward you in the end!"

This incident broke poor Raidas' heart. He left Ghanshyam's house and went to seek Birbal's help. Raidas narrated the entire incident to Birbal and said, "Please help me teach the miser merchant a suitable lesson."

Birbal empathised with the poet and suggested that he trick the merchant. Raidas liked Birbal's idea and went to meet his friend, Mayadas, who happily agreed to help him.

As per the plan, Mayadas sent a dinner invitation to the miserly merchant. The invitation promised that the guests would be served several delicacies in utensils made of gold and silver, which they could take back home after dinner.

Greedy Ghanshyam gladly accepted the invitation and arrived at Mayadas' house for dinner.

Ghanshyam was surprised to see that there were no other guests there except Birbal and him. Birbal and Mayadas kept conversing for a long time, and there was no mention of dinner. Finally, Ghanshyam said to Mayadas, "I am hungry, let us please eat!"

Mayadas smiled and replied, "I invited you here because I wanted some company, but I never intended to serve you any food."

Ghanshyam realised that he had been tricked. At that moment, Raidas entered the room. Birbal confronted the merchant for cheating Raidas. Ghanshyam realised his mistake and immediately apologised. He even gifted his necklace to Raidas as the pending reward.

Raidas thanked Birbal for his immense help. Mayadas then treated both of them to a fabulous dinner.

The Skinny Goat

One afternoon, Akbar and Birbal were having a lavish meal. Just as they finished eating, Birbal remarked, "Pardon me, Your Highness! But, you've gained some weight."

Akbar was quick to reply, "You're right, Birbal! It is because we're offered the most lavish meals, prepared by the best chefs, with the best and richest ingredients! I am bound to gain some weight!"

However, Birbal insisted, "I don't think it's the meals, Your Majesty! You're gaining weight because you have no worries or concerns at the moment."

Akbar retorted, "I disagree with you, Birbal! Even an animal can get fat if it is fed well."

Birbal didn't argue further, but he wanted to prove his point to the emperor, and so, he thought of a wise plan.

The next day, Birbal brought a healthy goat to the palace. Akbar understood what Birbal was trying to do and ordered the best of the royal servants to take care of it. For the next one month, both ensured that the goat was pampered and fed well.

A few weeks later, Emperor Akbar arrived to check on the goat and realised that instead of gaining weight, the goat had become skinnier.

He asked Birbal, "Are you not feeding the goat well? It has lost weight and become skinny!"

Birbal replied, "The goat has been fed very well, Your Highness! But I tied it near a lion's cage, and hence, due to its fear and worry, it has not gained any weight, and in fact, it has lost weight!"

Akbar realised that Birbal was right, and that living a stress-free life is the best tonic for being healthy.

The Miser's Treasure

Ghasita Lal was a miser who kept all his money in a wooden box. One day, when he returned home, he saw that his house was on fire. He screamed, "Somebody save the money box kept in my cupboard."

Ghasita Lal's neighbour, Ramkhilawan said, "I will help you but I will keep whatever I like and return the rest to you."

Ghasita Lal agreed. Ramkhilawan went inside the burning house and retrieved the box. He then told Ghasita Lal, "I choose to give you the box and I will keep all the money."

The two neighbours started arguing. When they saw Birbal there, they asked him to settle their dispute. Birbal said to Ramkhilawan, "You chose money, which is inside the box. So, according to the agreement, you must give it back to Ghasita Lal."

Ramkhilawan was speechless and returned the box to Ghasitalal. Upon Birbal's suggestion, Ghasita Lal gave a modest reward to Ramkhilawan for saving the box.

Counting Turns in the Street

One day, the Shah of Persia wrote to Akbar, asking him a strange question, "Can you tell me how many turns each street in your kingdom has?" Akbar was baffled by such a query. He sent officials to count every turn on each street of his kingdom. Though it seemed impossible, the courtiers began making a list.

When Birbal arrived at the palace, he sensed that Akbar was anxious. He asked Akbar, "What are you so worried about, Jahapanah?"

Akbar narrated the incident. After hearing it, Birbal smiled and said, "But the answer is very simple, huzoor! Any street in the world can turn either left or right. There can only be two turns."

Akbar wrote back to the Shah of Persia with the correct answer, and praised Birbal for his intelligence.

The End of Birbal's Exile ✻

One day, Emperor Akbar was angry with Birbal due to a disagreement and roared, "Birbal! Leave right now and never step foot on this country's soil again. If you return, you will be hanged!"

Birbal bowed and left the court. Several days passed, and Akbar mellowed down. He realised that he had overreacted and began to miss Birbal's advice on state matters.

One day, Akbar spotted Birbal riding a chariot near the palace. He was pouring down loose soil stored at the back of the chariot. Akbar stopped him and asked, "How dare your disobey me, Birbal? And why are you pouring mud on the ground like this?"

Birbal replied, "I dare not disobey you, Your Majesty! I have brought this soil from the neighbouring kingdom, so that I don't step on this country's soil, and can still be of service to you."

Akbar laughed at Birbal's witty reply and re-appointed him in his court.

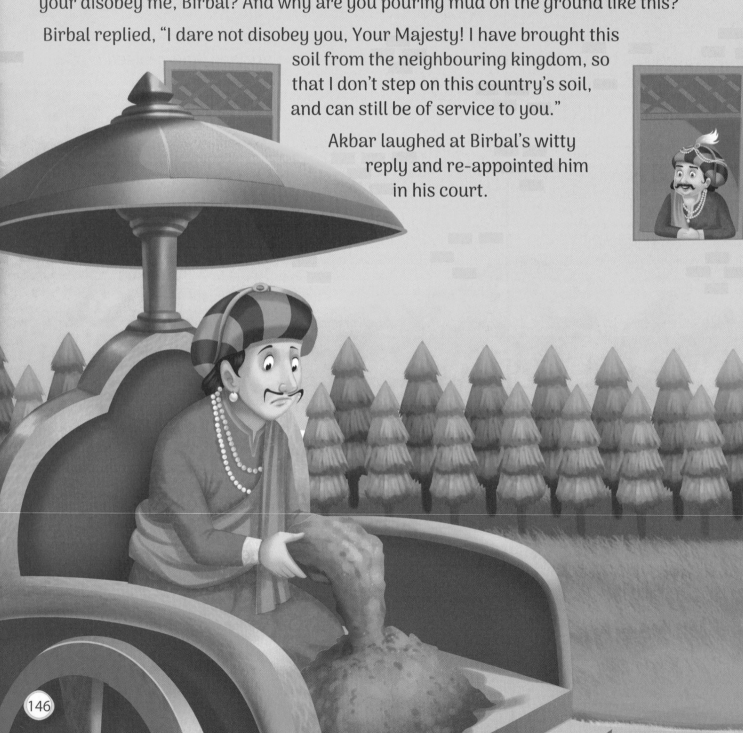

Birbal Tests a Scholar

A scholar once approached Emperor Akbar and proudly said, "Your Majesty! I have completed my education. I want Birbal to test my knowledge now." Akbar gladly accepted the request.

Birbal brought a huge jar and filled it with stones. He then asked the scholar, "Is there space for anything else in this jar?" The scholar quickly answered, "No!"

Next, Birbal filled the jar with small pebbles that filled the spaces between the stones. Birbal again asked, "Can I fill something else in the jar?" The scholar replied, "No, not anymore."

Then, Birbal put sand in the jar, and it filled the tiniest of empty spaces between the pebbles. Birbal explained, "Knowledge is like this jar. We think we've learned everything, but there's always something we can still learn in a lifetime."

The scholar bowed with respect and said, "You have indeed taught me a valuable lesson, Birbal!"

The New Head Priest

In Emperor Akbar's kingdom, there was a small temple situated at the top of a hill. The head priest of that temple was very old and respected by everyone.

After his demise, several priests expressed their desire to become the head priest. To avoid conflict, one of them suggested that they approach Birbal, who was famous for being wise and just. They met Birbal and said, "Please choose the new head priest for the temple."

Birbal asked all the priests to assemble at the bottom of the hill. Once everyone had arrived, Birbal announced, "The person who reaches the top of the temple first will be the new priest."

Birbal's odd criteria to choose the head priest surprised everyone.

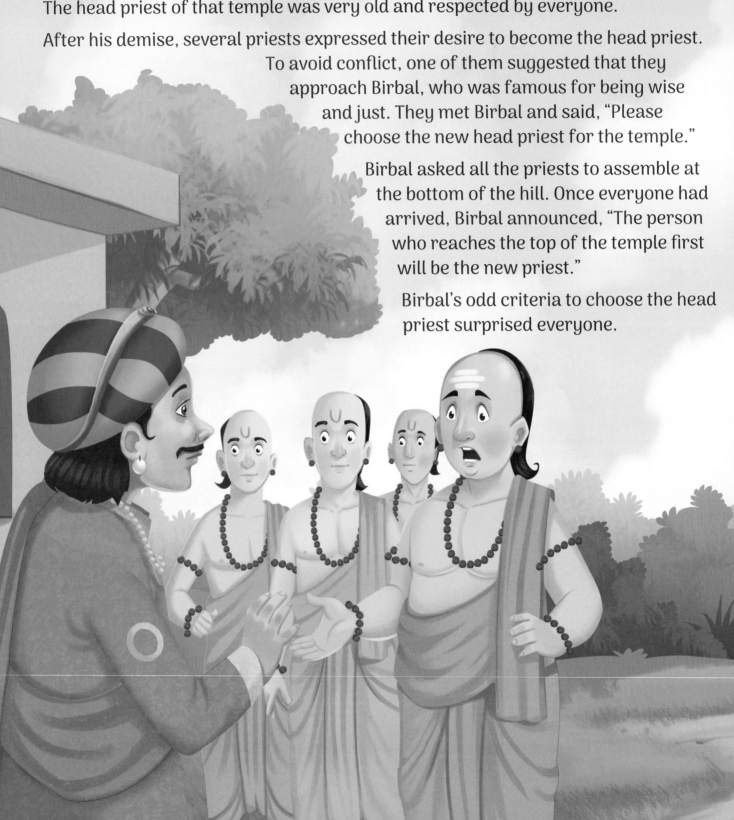

The path to the temple on the hill was steep and was littered with sharp rocks, thorns, and spiny bushes. All the priests started climbing the hill as quickly as they could. After some time, Birbal began to climb the hill. He was surprised to see a young priest lagging behind, with bruises on his hands and legs.

Birbal asked him, "What happened to you? You're late! All the other priests must have reached the temple already."

The wounded priest replied, "I was busy removing rocks and thorns from the path, so that devotees could reach the temple easily."

When Birbal and the young priest reached the temple, Birbal narrated his experience to the priests and then announced, "I declare this young man to be the new priest of this temple, as he put people's welfare above his desire to become the head priest."

The Mango Tree

One day, Birbal heard his neighbours, Rashid and Sadiq quarrelling with each other. When he enquired, Sadiq explained, "Birbal, I've nurtured this mango tree ever since it was a sapling. I deserve its fruits. However, Rashid is arguing that the tree belongs to him."

Birbal suggested, "Actually, it can belong to both of you. Pluck all its fruits and divide them equally. Further, you can cut down the tree and divide its wood too."

Rashid liked the idea and agreed to it. However, Sadiq cried, "No, Birbal! Let's not cut the tree. Rashid can have it entirely."

Birbal smiled and said, "We really can't stand to see our loved ones in pain. You win, Sadiq! You proved that you really care for this tree, and so, it belongs to you."

The Servant's Plight

One morning, Akbar was looking at himself in the mirror when he said to his servant, "Bring him to me!"

The servant immediately left the emperor's chambers but realised that Akbar didn't mention whom he was supposed to call. Since he was too terrified to ask the emperor, he met Birbal and asked for his help.

Birbal asked the servant, "What was emperor doing when he said this?" The servant replied, "He was looking at himself in the mirror." Birbal said, "It means that the emperor's hair has grown too long. He wants you to fetch the barber."

The servant returned with the barber. Akbar was surprised to see the barber and asked his servant, "I now realise that I forgot to mention the barber specifically. How did you know I asked for him?"

The servant explained how Birbal had helped him. Akbar smiled at Birbal's wisdom and praised his servant.

The Emperor's Touch

One day, an old lady approached Birbal and said, "My Lord! My son was a soldier who died in battle. Now, I'm all alone without his support. Please help me."

Birbal empathised with the old lady and suggested, "If you still have any of your son's belongings, give them to the emperor as a gift. He'll surely give you something valuable in return."

The next day, the old lady brought her son's sword to give to the emperor. Akbar examined it and said, "This is an ordinary sword and is full of rust. It is useless now. But I'll give you a few coins in exchange."

Birbal intervened, "Your Majesty! The sword might be rusted, but I believe that an emperor's touch can turn even rust into gold."

Akbar understood Birbal's hint. He immediately asked his officials to weigh the sword and give the old woman the same amount of gold.

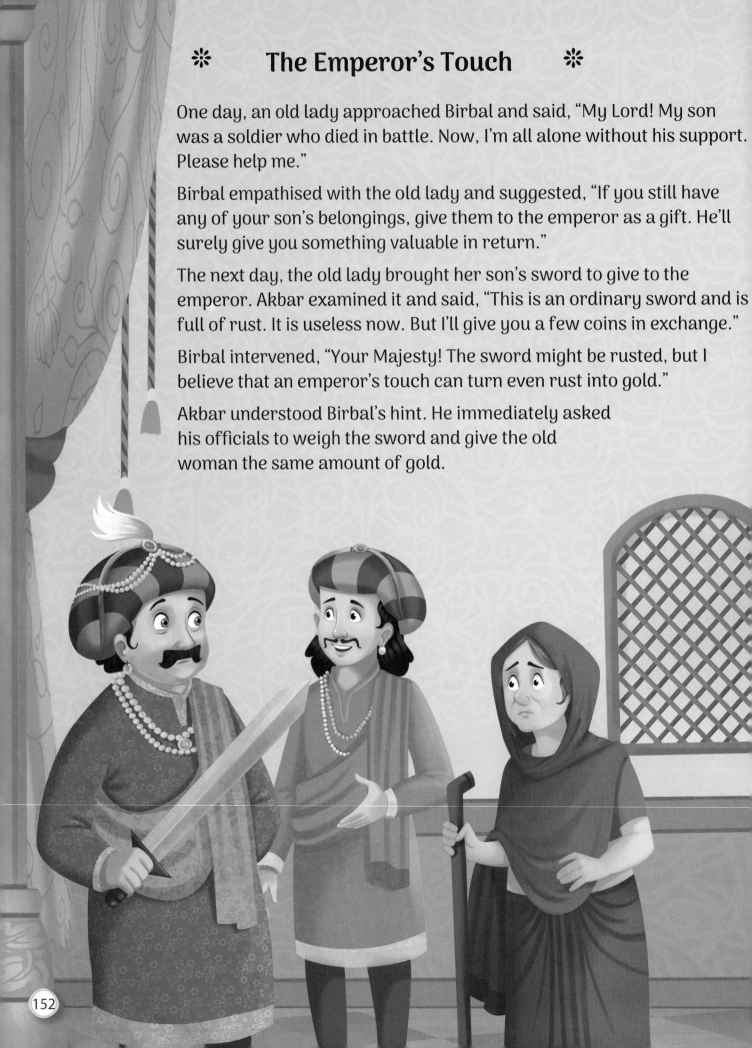

The Greedy Sage

There once lived a sage in Akbar's kingdom. One day, an old lady came to the sage's hut and said, "Guru ji! I'm leaving town for a few months. Can you keep my coins safe with you until I return?"

The sage replied, "I don't touch money. But if you want, you can bury your coins in the ground outside my hut."

The old lady did as instructed and left the town. However, when she returned after several months, she couldn't find her coins where she had buried them. When she asked the sage about it, he replied, "I have no knowledge about your coins."

The poor lady went to Birbal and narrated the entire incident. Birbal said that he could help her and asked her to act according to his plan.

He then went to the sage's hut with a bag of jewels and said, "Guru ji! Can you please take care of my jewels? I have to go visit my cousin in another city, and I can only trust a holy man like you."

The greedy sage was more than happy to help Birbal. But suddenly, the old woman entered the sage's hut, and he realised that she could spoil his plan by telling the truth. He pointed towards a corner and said to her, "My dear! Your coins are buried over there."

After the woman had successfully dug out her coins, Birbal's servant entered the hut and informed him, "My Lord! Your cousin has arrived at your house."
Birbal exclaimed, "Oh! I won't have to leave town now. So, I will not bother you anymore, Guru ji."

He then left the sage's hut without giving him the bag of jewels.

The Floating Palace

One night, Akbar dreamt about a floating palace. When the emperor woke up, he realised how much he would like to live in that unique palace.

He called for a conference with his architects and said, "I want you to build me a floating palace, just like the one in my dreams. It should not have any pillars to support it. Remember, I will punish you severely if you fail."

All the royal architects were shocked as they knew that it was an impossible task. However, none of them could tell the emperor that he was foolish for making such a weird demand.

Scared for their lives, all the architects approached Birbal, hoping he would have a solution. Birbal promised to help them.

The next day, Birbal arrived at Akbar's court looking really gloomy. When Akbar enquired about the reason for his sadness, Birbal replied, "Huzoor, I saw an amazing dream last night! I saw that I was an emperor with a lot of wealth and power. However, when I woke up, everything was gone. I feel sad about losing my fortune."

Akbar felt that Birbal was being unreasonable. He said, "Oh, Birbal! Don't be foolish. You can't expect all your dreams to come true."

Hearing this, Birbal smiled and remarked, "Your Majesty! Then I request you to consider the impracticality of your dream as well."

Akbar understood what Birbal was referring to and smiled. He called his architects and asked them to stop working on the floating palace. The royal architects thanked Birbal for saving their lives.

God's Plan

Akbar and Birbal were strolling in the royal garden one morning. The garden was home to many plants that bore delicious fruits and the most beautiful flowers.

Akbar noticed that the gardener was working meticulously, watering the plants and plucking weeds from around the trees. He said to Birbal, "We have to take great care of the plants. However, weeds grow everywhere on their own, even if we uproot them."

Birbal replied, "Your Majesty! These trees were planted by human hands and hence require care. Weeds, however, are planted by God. Anything planted by God is being taken care of by Him and hence doesn't require human efforts."

Akbar praised the depth of Birbal's philosophy, and appreciated the beauty of nature.

The Mysterious Painter

An artist once came to the royal palace and said to Akbar, "Your Majesty! You have a majestic palace. Can I paint it on my canvas?"

Akbar was flattered by the artist's remark and gladly agreed to his request. The artist was given access to the palace. He painted several paintings of the palace and ensured that he covered it from all possible angles.

When the artist completed all his paintings, he presented them in the court. Everybody was impressed with the level of detail and the sheer beauty of the paintings. Akbar rewarded him with several expensive gifts.

The artist asked for Akbar's permission to leave for his hometown, but Akbar insisted that he stay for a few more days, as he wanted to patronise the artist. The artist happily agreed. A few days later, the artist rushed to Akbar's court and complained, "Your Majesty! Someone has stolen all of my paintings and the gifts that you gave me from my chambers. Please help me!"

Akbar was furious as a theft in the royal palace was a matter of grave concern and embarrassment. He called his ministers and asked them to investigate the matter.

However, Birbal then revealed the truth, "Your Majesty! I was suspicious about this artist and so I sent my men to bring all his paintings and possessions to me. After going through his things, I'm sure that he's a spy sent by our enemies. He used the paintings as a cover to draw maps of our palace and help our enemies attack us."

Akbar and the other courtiers were shocked. Akbar ordered that the matter be investigated, and eventually, the artist confessed to being a spy. Akbar rewarded Birbal with several precious gifts and sent the spy to the royal prison.

✳ **The End**